City Lights

Lucy Nutlin

Contents

Original version—Chapter one

C hapter one

Walking alone on a cold Friday night was typical for me after long nights at the office trying to figure out who killed who and why so that maybe the poor victims' family and friends can find some sort of closure but that doesn't exist. That Victim will forever be remember in the most horrifying way. Why? Well because they were brutally murdered if they get lucky they aren't raped. Again poor souls and May they find peace within their 'afterlife' as some call it. For me well those faces, bodies, scars will forever haunt me in my dreams and even when I am in reality. That's my job solving and fighting crime not wanting the numbers of murders to rise. Too late for that I guess each day the streets of Chicago get worse and worse and soon everyone will be inside trying to survive. A wild dog they said. Just a wild dog who needs to learn some control killed the girl. What dog would tear a teenage girl to shred? No dog I know. Not here. The look on her pale bloody face still terrifies me. She was only fifteen, friends say she was out with some boy named Hector.

I walk to the apartment complex looking at the message Sampson sent me to make sure this is Hector's parents place. I wait for a couple minutes debating whether I should buzz again. As my finger goes to press it again the door opens revealing a very well dressed woman in her late forties. "Yes?" The woman asks eyeing me up and down. "Detective Ross I am here to investigate the case of Eliza. Sorry for the late timing but can I ask your son Hector a few questions regarding the case?" I look at the woman waiting for her response. "Sure but make it quick Hector has a game in the morning" I nod following her through the two bedroom apartment modernly decorated. "Hector there is a detective her to talk to you about Eliza" The woman says as she opens the door to I assume Hectors room which is very messy. "Where can we talk?"

As we sit in the kitchen with his mom present of course Hector begins to fidget. "Don't be nervous it will go by quick" I give a smile to calm him down but he just turns red. "So around what time did you last see Eliza?" I take out my notepad ready to jot down anything important. "Around...nine, ten I think she wanted to go outside and so I went back to get a drink"

"Was she drinking? Under the influence?"

"Yes she was a bit tipsy so I just left letting Juliet know"

"Who is Juliet?"

"Her best friend they are inseparable. Juliet wanted to keep an eye on her cause she hardly knows how to drink."

"So she gets easily drunk." I wrote that down to seem like half of this was important but it was hardly not. I take a sip of my sparkling water they offered me. "You said you left her around nine, ten right?" He nods "But the body was discovered at eight, how is that possible?" I look at the sheets of information to make sure I was correct. "Let me check my phone because I sent a text to Juliet-"He grabs his phone going through it. "Hector do you mind if I look through it? I could get a permit but-"He looks at his mom who nods. "Sure" I read through the most recent messages wanting to find something anything that will help me figure out what did this. I lied about the permit the firm doesn't want me to be in this case anymore they think it's an animal. "Okay thank you for your time." I give him back the phone when I find nothing. "No problem detective" The mother says following me to the door. As soon as I am out my phone rings. "Ross"

"It's me Sampson. Find anything?" I huff rummaging for my car keys. "Nope. I swear teens need to stop getting drunk" He laughs "we were like that once Morgan." I enter my car rolling my eyes. "Not me I was the geek who fangirled too much about Buffy the Vampire slayer"

"Well we'll just have to keep looking. Keep me posted."

"Alright goodnight"

"Goodnight..."

I arrive home which is just a one bedroom apartment filled with books and files of solved and unsolved cases. I tidy up the room waiting for the call wanting to get some work done, craving work. I turn to look at my clock It's not too late for some research. I crack open my laptop and just as I do that my phone begins to ring. "Ross." I say answering the phone. "Three theories" Sampson says as I grab a note pad and pen. "Which are?" Sampson sighs "Well they are very unusual and you might think I am out of my mind but here they go..." I roll my eyes as he struggles to tell me the 'foolish' theories. "Okay. So I did some research-"

"Just get to the point"

"Okay. Werewolves. I mean like look at the tearing of the skin and it was done at night werewolves!" I scoff at the overly excited Sampson. "You're crazy"

"I knew I shouldn't have told you! I thought you would understand considering you watched Buffy the Vampire slayer you'll under-stand."

"It's a show! Let me guess your other two theories are vampires and zombies" I say sarcastically but I think I was right. "C'mon Sam werewolves? Vampires? Zombies!? They don't exist" I look back at the information I found on the missing girl. "She did die at night but that doesn't mean it was a man turned wolf that is like I said crazy"

"It was just a theory that maybe things we believe are untrue are true. All I know is that something is not right about this. Goodnight again call me if you find anything"

"I will Sam go to sleep I think you need it." I say before hanging up. I stare at my laptop screen hoping that I get a bright idea that will solve this case but I get nothing.

The next morning two more dead bodies were found outside a bar called Los Labios Rojos. "Juliet sixteen and Hector sixteen." The cop said as I walk to the two bodies uncovering the blue cover. "Who the hell let these teenagers in this bar?!" I ask walking over to one of the cops. "Talk to the bouncer he was here all night looks a bit shaken up maybe it's the coffee he keeps on drinking" The cop said "Or maybe it's the fact that there are two teenagers who are dead right in front of him."

I walk to the bouncer who has crazy eyes. "Detective Ross. I am here to ask a few questions concerning the deaths of Juliet and Hector" He nods taking a sip of his coffee. "Would you prefer if we speak here or the coffee shop down the street?"

We make our way to the small coffee shop finding a spot in the corner. "So did you ever see these two during your shift?" I ask taking out the two pictures of Juliet and Hector before their death. "Yeah but I-I didn't let them come in the bar they looked to young and the fake ID were well n-not very good" He grabs the cup of coffee spilling some due to his shaky hand. "Okay so you didn't let them in the club then what were they doing?" I am not certain that this bouncer is telling the complete truth for all I know he could be dealing with a hangover and was too drunk last night to remember who these kids were. Maybe he just wants me to leave so he is giving me random information. "I don't know they were kissing and giggling when they were in line when I told them they couldn't come in they went to the alley and never came back." I nod jotting it all down. "Around what time was this?" I look up from my notebook as he tries to go back to the day. "I don't know past midnight" I nod. "Thank for you time-"I begin to say but he cuts me off. "I heard something it may sound crazy but it was a growl but not a wild dog growl it was too low and it sent chills down my spine." I thought back to what Sampson had said to me the night before which is again crazy.

"He heard a growl I seriously think he was drunk when he was working." I say as Sampson smiles. "We are going take the bodies down to get them checked up which won't take long they both look like the first victim." I nod as they take them away. "We spoke to Hector yesterday and today he turns up dead..." I sigh. "Teens are being murdered for who knows what reason" I look down at my phone. "Have they told their parents?" Sampson shakes his head. "No"

"Great. Now I have to give her the horrible news who is going to talk to Juliet's parents?"

"I will"

"Okay"

The day seemed darker as I saw his mother outside with a cup of steaming tea worry in her eyes. "Detective I have been meaning to call you Hector hasn't been home since last night." She says I sigh and her facial expression changes. "What happened? Please tell me you know where my baby boy is" Tears begin to overflow her eyes. "I am very sorry Hector turned up this morning. I am so sorry for your loss" As soon as those words came out of my mouth she dropped her cup shattering it. "No." She clutches her heart sobbing. "Again I am very sorry we will find who did this and end it" She nods sniffling. "I need to be alone right now" She says I nod walking back to my car.

"How did it go?"

"Not good they cried and cried I mean it was their youngest daughter"

"Same here Hector was her only hope she is now alone poor people"

"That's why we have to figure out who the hell did this"

"I have to go do some research I am going to talk to a few kids who went to school with them and who were there the day Eliza was killed"

"Okay"

I throw the keys on the counter not very satisfied with what the teens had to say about that night half of them were too drunk to remember what happened and the other half weren't invited so that leaves me with nothing. I didn't even get to interview Juliet who must have known something. There is just too many blank spaces in this case.

"Detective Ross speaking"

"We closed the case it was a wild wolf that was loose. We can all sleep well tonight if anything comes up the same it is no longer our problem. Animal control has it covered." The chief says "So a wild animal killed three close friends two on the same night and one before that? It must be a really smart wolf" He sighs "We can't do anything. Don't do anything...it's an order" I sigh "Don't do anything got it" I say before hanging up.

I can finally take some time for myself until another case pops up. I lay back on the tub filled with warm water shutting my eyes.

I open my eyes as I hear a high pitched scream and a low growl sending chills down my spine. I get up quickly grabbing a robe, my gun, before running down the steps down to the alley. "Help is on the way!" I yell as the girl is still screaming looking into a dark corner where all you can see are electric blue eyes and sharp white teeth. "Stay behind me." I tell the girl who looks about nineteen. I point my gun at the creature wishing I had brought my phone. "Run. Get Help" I command the scared girl who ran for her life but the animal didn't seem to care about it. Its eyes were on me. I slowly back away but it growls making me shiver. Then something I didn't expect happened. It was shifting, all I heard were bones cracking and groaning and moaning. "I won't hurt you" A deep masculine voice tells me. "I promise I am not the one who is killing these innocent people" I stand there shocked for a moment before responding. "I am dreaming this is all fake right? I mean werewolves do not exist!" I bite my lip trying to process this whole thing. "This is a dream. Get it together Morgan!" I laugh as the man comes closer. "No this is not a dream this is real Morgan." I feel like I have been punch in the gut when he comes into view. His eyes. His lips. His jawline. He looks like a god.

"Stay back" I warn. "Okay relax" He puts his hands up in defense not liking the gun that is pointed to his head. "How do you know my name? Who are you?" I ask raising my eyebrow. "Detectives gotta love them" He says his emerald green eyes showing a hint of humor. "I see you on the papers the case with the three dead teens." He says putting me back into reality. "You killed them? And you were about to kill that poor girl" I look down at my robe as a gust of wind makes my body shiver. "No I don't kill. Well I don't kill innocent people I am not like the rest. Not anymore." The cold air finally begins to hit me. "Your cold. We should go somewhere else" He suggests. "Totally I am going to take a freaking werewolf to my apartment! Like that isn't crazy!" I roll my eyes as he smiles. "I don't want you to freeze to death." I scoff. "Fine lets go insi-"Before I know it I am in a forest alone before he comes back. "What the hell! I have work tomorrow!" He hands me some clothes. "Change and we'll discuss it later"

"Discuss it later! What is there to discuss!? I need to go home! I have a job and a life." I look down at the flannel and jeans before looking back up at him. "Why am I here?" I ask as he continues to stare me down. "Change and we'll discuss it later" He repeats in the same tone.

"I am not changing here."

"Fine follow me."

Original version-Chapter two

I follow him to an old shed that looks like it's about to fall at any point. "Scream if you find anything" He says "I have my-"I begin to say realizing my gun was no longer with me. "Yeah I took your gun when we came here" I swear under my breath before entering the shed to change because it's cold and I don't want to be naked in front of a stranger. "Stupid wolf-man" I mumble slipping into my jeans. "I can hear you" I roll my eyes before coming outside. "You forgot the shoes" I look down at my bare feet. When I look up he was walking to I don't know where. I had to jog to keep up with him. "Where are we going?" He stops making me collide with his back. "You'll see" I fix the hair that smacked my face.

We make are way to a very large mansion that looks surprisingly cozy. "This is where you will be spending the rest of your days until we figure out what to do with you." He says I stop in my tracks. "I am not staying here I need to go home" I look behind me and see this as my chance to run as his back is turned to me. "You can't go home. Not yet" I turn ready to run anywhere but two large hands catch me throwing me over his shoulder. "Nope not going to happen" I huff. "I wish this was a dream" I huff as my hair falls down on my face.

"Why is there a human here?" Some dude I don't know asks "You'll find out later" The man says while I am still over his shoulder. "I ask myself that every second I am here" I say as we pass the guy who I can only see his feet. "We are going to meet my uncles Micas and Lucas and then" He hesitates before finishing his sentence. "My brother" He says putting me down. "No more trying to run I can hear your heartbeat so don't bother tip toeing" I huff a house full of werewolves that all have super senses it is going to be hard as hell to escape this place and go home.

We walk towards two double doors. "Uncles I bring Morgan Ross"
He says opening the door where two men sit drinking some whisky.
"The famous Morgan Ross?" One says eyeing me with his ocean blue
eyes. "You look just like your mother" The other says catching me
off guard. "My mother?" I ask. I never met my mother my dad raised
me. "You Morgan are a legend that will stop this war" Blue eyes says
smiling. "Why? I am just human" They both smile "So you think"
Why did this have to happen to me! I mean it's cool and all being in a
room full of werewolves but not when they can kill you in a second.

"I am Micas by the way" Blue eyes says smiling. "And I am Lucas"
The other says. I nod giving a smile back well forcing a smile back.
"Cain where is your brother Jaspar?" Lucas asks and at that moment
a handsome man comes into the room flashing a smile. "Speak of
the devil" The green eyed man also known as Cain says. "Where is
she?" He asks until his eyes land on me. "I'm Jaspar. You must be the
legendary Morgan" I nod "So I have been told"

After a few moments where I catch Jaspar staring at me with a smirk.
"So I need information I can't trust you guys I just met you. I need
to find out who is killing those teens and why. I also need to know
why I am so important to you guys. If you don't give me answers I

won't be so easy to tame." I say giving them a stern look. "Feisty I like her" Jasper comment earning a glare from Cain. "Fine will give you answers" Micas says. "You might want to sit down for this" I roll my eyes crossing my arms across my chest leaning against the velvet wall. "We are not the killers the Vampires are they make it look like a wild dog or in this case we killed them but we didn't they just want to scare our kind outside the kingdom. They want to turn our kind against us so they can then kill them and rule the city." I raise an eyebrow "Vampires? Really what is next fairies and unicorns?!" I scoff. "No they are fake" Lucas says grinning. "Keep going" Morgan commands wanting all the answers spinning in her head to be solved. "We need you. Your mother was the best Luna we could have asked for she was strong, beautiful, and graceful. She let us down the day she had an affair with a Vampire resulting in you the very first hybrid." I was taken back by his words. "Wait so my real father is a vampire and my mother was a Luna? What is a Luna?" I ask "A Luna is a pack leader we have no Luna at the moment but we need one and I think you are the perfect one for the job I mean it's in your blood." I take deep breath. "I don't have any super powers or whatever you call them" I look down at my normal self. "Not yet we haven't done the ritual you usually have when you are a pup but since you were raised with humans then we have to do it now that you are an adult." Lucas says "But for now I am guessing you are overwhelmed with all this so I will send someone to take you to your bedroom" I run my hand through my hair. "I can't believe this I have to go to work in a couple hours!" I say looking out the window as the sun has already risen.

"Here you go" Cain says opening the door for me. "Thank you" I step inside the enormous room. "My room is two doors down if you have any trouble" He informs me before leaving me to gawk at the room before me. This is nothing compared to my apartment back in the city. I snoop around the room opening the closet filled with gorgeous expensive looking dresses. "Those were your mothers" I turn around to see Lucas standing in the doorway. "Was this her room?" I ask already knowing the answer. "Yes I thought it would suit you. You look just like her" I look into the mirror picturing an older me. "Where you guys close?" I ask earning a small smile from him. "Yes we were she was my first love I was in charge of protecting her while she found her mate; our alpha." I nod touching the soft red silk on the bed. "We are your family now Morgan now more than ever we must stick together to defend ourselves to save humanity and our kind"

After he left I went took a shower this time with no interruptions. I need a plan to contact Sampson that I am all right if the girl did do as I told her then help should have been on its way. Maybe she was too scared and now my boss will think I am a screw up who didn't show up to work today. I can't sleep even though my bones ache and I am tired but I need to do something. I can't just let them control my life. I go over to the closet to pick out some jeans and a t-shirt but all I saw were dresses and skirts. I keep searching until I found two double door behind a rack of dresses. I opened it to find a walk in closet filled with more dresses, shoes and pants! I have never been so happy to see a pair of pant. "Finally"

I walk down the wooden steps wanting to get more information knowing that the one they had given me wasn't the whole truth. Something still didn't make me trust them. I need to find a library or something to research these creatures which now I am one of them. I am not human...I touch my face which feels the same. "Newbie" A voice says I look up and see a tall blonde guy with grey eyes with a giant grin on his face. "That is not my name"

"I know it's the legendary Morgan Ross!" He exclaims. "No it's just Morgan"

"Okay 'just Morgan' my name is Josh" He says with a playful grin. "So I heard you are doing the ritual" He says like he didn't just try to kill me with annoyance. "Yes I am. I don't know why this is any of your business" He smiles at my remark. "Feisty. I like you." I smile liking this somewhat of a compliment. "What is the ritual anyways?" I ask hoping he will be an easy way to answers. "You have to stand mostly naked in front of the pack and say some vows then they make you drink something it hurts like a bitch. After that you transform or shift and we all go in and celebrate"

"Mostly naked?"

"Yup'"

"I have to drink something?" What if it's poison? "Yeah I think it like activates your animal side" I nod dreading this ritual. "When does it take place?" He thinks for a while. "As soon as you are ten but for you they will wait 'till midnight" I take a deep breath. "Okay"

"Don't get nervous."

"I don't get nervous"

"You look nervous"

"I do not"

"Do to"

"Do no-okay I feel like a five year old doing this with you. I have another question"

"Shoot"

"Do you happen to know if you guys have a library?" He sighs "I thought you were going to say bar but yeah we do but it's off limits only Cain can go in there and he is really moody" I furrow my eyebrows. "Cain moody? I may have just met him like a couple hours ago but he seems nice" Josh scoffs. "When he is with you but in battle or just anywhere he has a scowl on his face." He says in a low voice. "I feel bad for whoever is going to be his mate"

"What is a mate?" I ask boy do I feel dumb for asking so many questions. "You need to go to werewolf 101 'cause you don't know shiz" He grabs my arm dragging me down the halls. "I am going to be your teacher" I roll my eyes at him as he makes me sit down on one of the many couches. "So lesson one-Mates." Josh begins to say as I try my best not to laugh at this. "A mate is someone you are meant to be with literally the moon goddess chooses a perfect match for you. It is amazing-so I have been told-they say it's more a curse then a gift. You die when they die basically. Unless you get a second chance." I feel like I should be jotting this down from how important he is making all this sound.

"I see you are teaching our upcoming pack member the ropes" Micas says walking into the room. "Morgan the ritual will take place during the next full moon which will be next week" I let out a breath of relief. "So I can go home?" I say with a small bit of hope. "No" Another voice says I turn and see Cain standing in the door way. "Why not?" I get up from my seat a little annoyed. "Because I said so and what I say I want done gets done you are staying here and that's final" I scoff as he storms out the room. "What's up with him?" I ask Micas who has a grin on his face. "He has been moody all this week ever since he went to the city to look for you" Micas informs me. "That's unusual" I say getting a grin from Josh and Micas. "Morgan come with me I want to show you something" Jaspar says coming into the room. "Okay..." I look back at Josh and Micas as Jaspar takes my hand leading me somewhere. "Where are we going?" I ask as we go through halls and halls filled with paintings that looks very expensive. "You'll see" He says looking back at me with a kind smile. "I am not good with surprises Jaspar" I say as we go through two glass doors and into a magnificent garden. "Wow this place is beautiful" I gasp as I see all the exotic flowers beautifully arranged. "It is very beautiful" Jaspar says looking at me. "If you ever need to escape mentally you can always come here." It's nice to know that at least one brother is nice to me. "Thank you" I say yawning afterwards. "You must be exhausted with all the news you just got" I nod as I feel my eye begin to droop. "I have never-"I yawn again."-Been so sleepy in my entire life" I stretch not in the mood to walk all the way back. "Let me help you" Jaspar says picking me up bridal style. "What are you doing" I say not trusting this guy I just met. "You are too tired to walk so I'll take you to your room" He says and the rest was all mumbles.

I woke up to loud yelling and stuff being thrown on the ground. I look around the room looking for a weapon any weapon I can take to protect myself. I open the door walking over to the stairs where I see him. Cain but it looks nothing like him his eyes are black his teeth are-I turn away for the first time I am terrified. "Morgan come with me" Josh says making Cain turn swiftly growling the moment Josh's hands landed on me. "Now lock your door and don't come out until morning" I do as he say before Josh goes back down to calm a very angry Cain.

As I lay on my bed I felt something stir inside me and urge to go somewhere. I ignored it but it kept growing and growing until I no longer felt like I had any control over my actions and I found myself outside Cain's room. I lift my hand to knock but the door flies open revealing a shirtless Cain his breath heavy and his eyes dark. "I-" I begin to say but his lips crash onto mine sending chills down my spine from how good it felt. "Mine" Cain says as he throws me on his bed showering me with kisses. "Yours" I reply not feeling like myself. Soon our clothes our on the floor and our bodies are where they belong. He soon begins to kiss my neck before I feel two sharp fangs on it. He bites down making me scream. "You belong to me now"

I wake up in a sweaty bed with beads of sweat coming out of my forehead. My heart is pounding against my chest. I get up and go in the shower turning the water icy cold as I feel like I am in a heated room. "Fuck" I say stepping into the cold shower. "Fuck" I fall on the floor knees against my chest thinking back to the dream making me more heated than before. I rip my clothes off sitting naked trying to figure out what the hell is happening to me. Once I finally cooled off I changed into a loose white top and jeans walking bare foot to the garden but then getting an idea. I need to escape I can't live here and fight a war for people I barely met. I look around the house making sure no one is out and about. I open the back door leading to the garden where I climb the tall wall.

I hit the ground on my feet sprinting my way to the only 'secure' place in this damn forest I know the shed. I finally reach it out of breath I look all around as the birds are beginning to die down. I slip through the doors finding a match lighting it before searching for a candle. I find an old dusty candle lighting it up looking for things mostly weapons. I find a stick making it into a spear hiding it by some old tools. I toss the non-threatening tools to one side. What the hell is a shed doing in the middle of the forest any ways? I rummage through all the boxes and other stuff before finding a cute decorated box filled with letters from Catalina to a man named Victor. Curiosity takes over me as I grab the first letter trying not to rip it.

My Dearest Victor,

Oh how I dread the day we part. Each day I leave you my heart aches I know I am destined to someone it is natural for me to have a mate and when I find that mate I will reject him. We can re-unite the my kind with your kind I know they will be angry at first but my love we will go through this together and we will live for eternity as our love will never die. They will hate me for backing out on their new Alpha but I know that you will make a magnificent leader. I can't wait to see you again. I don't know what excuse to make this time maybe my dress ripped and I need to get it fixed. Or maybe I need a new pair of shoes and I'll send the maids to go fetch them and I'll sneak away where we can meet by the waterfall. I hope no one finds these letters. I have no idea if I should send them to you I do have some important news to tell you I don't know if I should tell you now or wait to tell you in person. They will soon know in a couple months. Oh I can't wait to tell you! I think I should just tell you now! Oh my dearest love, I love you so very much and I know you will be as happy as I am to tell you we just made history my lovely Victor we are having a baby and I have a feeling it's a baby girl. I am in love with the name Morgan what do you think. My love she will be the daughter of two loving parents and most importantly two great leaders from two very important kinds. She will be powerful and strong. She will end this war once and for all and maybe if we are lucky we will get to be a happy family. Like I had always wanted a family that I chose to have not that was destined to be. I just want to let you know how much I love you and absolutely adore you but I know you know that.

Forever with you,

Catalina

Chapter One

Chapter one

Walking alone on a cold Friday night was typical for me after long nights at the office trying to figure out who killed who and why so that maybe the poor victims' family and friends can find some sort of closure but that doesn't exist. That Victim will forever be remembered in the most horrifying way. Why? Well because they were brutally murdered . Again, poor souls and May they find peace within their 'afterlife' as some call it. For me well those faces, bodies, scars will forever haunt me in my dreams and even when I am in reality. That's my job solving and fighting crime not wanting the numbers of murders to rise. Too late for that I guess each day the streets of Chicago get worse and worse and soon everyone will be inside trying to survive. A wild dog they said. Just a wild dog who needs to learn some control killed the girl. What dog would tear a teenage girl to shred? No dog I know. Not here. The look on her pale bloody face still terrifies me. She was only fifteen, friends say she was out with some boy named Hector.

I walk to the apartment complex looking at the message Sampson sent me to make sure this is Hector's parents place. I wait for a couple minutes debating whether I should buzz again. As my finger goes to press it again the door opens revealing a very well dressed woman in her late forties. "Yes?" The woman asks eyeing me up and down. "Detective Ross I am here to investigate the case of Eliza. Sorry for the late timing but can I ask your son Hector a few questions regarding the case?" I look at the woman waiting for her response. "Sure, but make it quick Hector has a game in the morning" I nod following her through the two-bedroom apartment modernly decorated. "Hector there is a detective her to talk to you about Eliza" The woman says as she opens the door to I assume Hectors room which is very messy. "Where can we talk?"

As we sit in the kitchen with his mom present of course Hector begins to fidget. "Don't be nervous it will go by quick" I give a smile to calm him down but he just turns red. "So around what time did you last see Eliza?" I take out my notepad ready to jot down anything important. "Around...nine, ten I think she wanted to go outside and so I went back to get a drink"

"Was she drinking? Was she drunk?"

"Yes, she was a bit tipsy so I just left letting Juliet know"

"Who is Juliet?"

"Her best friend they are inseparable. Juliet wanted to keep an eye on her cause she hardly knows how to drink."

"So, she gets easily drunk." I wrote that down to seem like half of this was important but it was hardly not. I take a sip of my sparkling water they offered me. "You said you left her around nine, ten, right?" He nods "But the body was discovered at eight, how is that possible?" I look at the sheets of information to make sure I was correct. "Let me check my phone because I sent a text to Juliet- "He grabs his phone going through it. "Hector, do you mind if I look through it? I could get a permit but- "He looks at his mom who nods. "Sure" I read through the most recent messages wanting to find something anything that will help me figure out what did this. I lied about the permit the firm doesn't want me to be in this case anymore they think it's an animal. "Okay thank you for your time." I give him back the phone when I find nothing. "No problem detective" The mother says following me to the door. As soon as I am out my phone rings. "Ross"

"Well we'll just have to keep looking. Keep me posted."

"Alright goodnight"

"Goodnight..."

I arrive home which is just a one bedroom apartment filled with books and files of solved and unsolved cases. I tidy up the room waiting for the call wanting to get some work done, craving work. I turn to look at my clock It's not too late for some research. I crack open my laptop and just as I do that my phone begins to ring. "Ross." I say answering the phone. "Three theories" Sampson says as I grab a note pad and pen. "Which are?" Sampson sighs "Well they are very unusual and you might think I am out of my mind but here they go..." I roll my eyes as he struggles to tell me the 'foolish' theories. "Okay. So, I did some research- "

"Just get to the point"

"Okay. Werewolves. I mean like look at the tearing of the skin and it was done at night werewolves!" I scoff at the overly excited Sampson. "You're crazy"

"I knew I shouldn't have told you! I thought you would understand considering you watched Buffy the Vampire slayer you'll understand."

"It's a show! Let me guess your other two theories are vampires and zombies" I say sarcastically but I think I was right. "C'mon Sam werewolves? Vampires? Zombies!? They don't exist" I look back at the information I found on the missing girl. "She did die at night but that doesn't mean it was a man turned wolf that is like I said crazy"

"It was just a theory that maybe things we believe are untrue are true. All I know is that something is not right about this. Goodnight again call me if you find anything"

"I will Sam go to sleep I think you need it." I say before hanging up. I stare at my laptop screen hoping that I get a bright idea that will solve this case but I get nothing.

The next morning two more dead bodies were found outside a bar called Los Labios Rojos. "Juliet sixteen and Hector sixteen." The cop said as I walk to the two bodies uncovering the blue cover. "Who the hell let these teenagers in this bar?!" I ask walking over to one of the cops. "Talk to the bouncer he was here all night looks a bit shaken up maybe it's the coffee he keeps on drinking" The cop said "Or maybe it's the fact that there are two teenagers who are dead right in front of him."

I walk to the bouncer who has crazy eyes. "Detective Ross. I am here to ask a few questions concerning the deaths of Juliet and Hector" He nods taking a sip of his coffee. "Would you prefer if we speak here or the coffee shop down the street?"

We make our way to the small coffee shop finding a spot in the corner. "So, did you ever see these two during your shift?" I ask taking out the two pictures of Juliet and Hector before their death. "Yeah but I-I didn't let them come in the bar they looked too young and the fake ID were well n-not very good" He grabs the cup of coffee spilling some due to his shaky hand. "Okay so you didn't let them in the club then what were they doing?" I am not certain that this bouncer is telling the complete truth for all I know he could be dealing with a hangover and was too drunk last night to remember who these kids were. Maybe he just wants me to leave so he is giving me random information. "I don't know they were kissing and giggling when they were in line when I told them they couldn't come in they went to the alley and never came back." I nod jotting it all down. "Around what time was this?" I look up from my notebook as he tries to go back to the day. "I don't know past midnight" I nod. "Thank for you time-"I begin to say but he cuts me off. "I heard something it may sound crazy but it was a growl but not a wild dog growl it was too low and it sent chills down my spine." I thought back to what Sampson had said to me the night before which is again crazy.

"He heard a growl I seriously think he was drunk when he was working." I say as Sampson smiles. "We are going take the bodies down to get them checked up which won't take long they both look like the first victim." I nod as they take them away. "We spoke to Hector yesterday and today he turns up dead..." I sigh. "Teens are being murdered for who knows what reason" I look down at my phone. "Have they told their parents?" Sampson shakes his head. "No"

"Great. Now I have to give her the horrible news who is going to talk to Juliet's parents?"

"I will"

"Okay"

The day seemed darker as I saw his mother outside with a cup of steaming tea worry in her eyes. "Detective I have been meaning to call you Hector hasn't been home since last night." She says I sigh and her facial expression changes. "What happened? Please tell me you know where my baby boy is" Tears begin to overflow her eyes. "I am very sorry Hector turned up this morning. I am so sorry for your loss" As soon as those words came out of my mouth she dropped her cup shattering it. "No." She clutches her heart sobbing. "Again, I am very sorry we will find who did this and end it" She nods sniffling. "I need to be alone right now" She says I nod walking back to my car.

"How did it go?"

"Not good they cried and cried I mean it was their youngest daughter"

"Same here Hector was her only hope she is now alone poor people"

"That's why we have to figure out who the hell did this"

"I have to go do some research I am going to talk to a few kids who went to school with them and who were there the day Eliza was killed"

"Okay"

I throw the keys on the counter not very satisfied with what the teens had to say about that night half of them were too drunk to remember what happened and the other half weren't invited so that leaves me with nothing. I didn't even get to interview Juliet who must have known something. There is just too many blank spaces in this case.

"Detective Ross speaking"

"We closed the case it was a wild wolf that was loose. We can all sleep well tonight if anything comes up the same it is no longer our problem. Animal control has it covered." The chief says "So a wild animal killed three close friends two on the same night and one before that? It must be a really smart wolf" He sighs "We can't do anything. Don't do anything...it's an order" I sigh "Don't do anything got it" I say before hanging up.

I can finally take some time for myself until another case pops up. I lay back on the tub filled with warm water shutting my eyes.

I open my eyes as I hear a high-pitched scream and a low growl sending chills down my spine. I get up quickly grabbing a robe, my gun, before running down the steps down to the alley. "Help is on the way!" I yell as the girl is still screaming looking into a dark corner where all you can see are electric blue eyes and sharp white teeth. "Stay behind me." I tell the girl who looks about nineteen. I point my gun at the creature wishing I had brought my phone. "Run. Get Help" I command the scared girl who ran for her life but the animal didn't seem to care about it. Its eyes were on me. I slowly back away but it growls making me jump. Then something I didn't expect happened. It was shifting, all I heard were bones cracking and groaning and moaning. "I won't hurt you" A deep masculine voice tells me. "I promise I am not the one who is killing these innocent people" I stand there shocked for a moment before responding. "I am dreaming this is all fake, right? I mean werewolves do not exist!" I bite my lip trying to process this whole thing. "This is a dream. Get it together Morgan!" I laugh as the man comes closer. "No this is not a dream this is real Morgan." I feel like I have been punch in the gut when he comes into view. His eyes. His lips. His jawline. He looks like a god.

"Stay back" I warn. "Okay relax" He puts his hands up in defense not liking the gun that is pointed to his head. "How do you know my name? Who are you?" I ask raising my eyebrow. "Detectives gotta love them" He says his emerald green eyes showing a hint of humor. "I see you on the papers the case with the three dead teens." He says putting me back into reality. "You killed them? And you were about to kill that poor girl" I look down at my robe as a gust of wind makes my body shiver. "No I don't kill. Well I don't kill innocent people I am not like the rest. Not anymore." The cold air finally begins to hit me. "Your cold. We should go somewhere else" He suggests. "Totally I am going to take a freaking werewolf to my apartment! Like that isn't crazy!" I roll my eyes as he smiles. "I don't want you to freeze to death." I scoff. "Fine let's go insi- "Before I know it I am in a forest alone before he comes back. "What the hell! I have work tomorrow!" He hands me some clothes. "Change and we'll discuss it later"

"Discuss it later! What is there to discuss!? I need to go home! I have a job and a life." I look down at the flannel and jeans before looking back up at him. "Why am I here?" I ask as he continues to stare me down. "Change and we'll discuss it later" He repeats in the same tone. "I am not changing here."

"Fine follow me."

Chapter Two

Chapter two

I follow him to an old shed that looks like it's about to fall at any point. "Scream if you find anything" He says "I have my- "I begin to say realizing my gun was no longer with me. "Yeah I took your gun when we came here" I swear under my breath before entering the shed to change because it's cold and I don't want to be naked in front of a stranger. "Stupid wolf-man" I mumble slipping into my jeans. "I can hear you" I roll my eyes before coming outside. "You forgot the shoes" I look down at my bare feet. When I look up he was walking to I don't know where. I had to jog to keep up with him. "Where are, we going?" He stops making me collide with his back. "You'll see" I fix the hair that smacked my face.

We make are way to a very large mansion that looks surprisingly cozy.
"This is where you will be spending the rest of your days until we
figure out what to do with you." He says I stop in my tracks. "I am
not staying here I need to go home" I look behind me and see this as
my chance to run as his back is turned to me. "You can't go home.
Not yet" I turn ready to run anywhere but two large hands catch me
throwing me over his shoulder. "Nope not going to happen" I huff.
"I wish this was a dream" I huff as my hair falls on my face.

"Why is there a human here?" Some dude I don't know asks "You'll
find out later" The man says while I am still over his shoulder. "I ask
myself that every second I am here" I say as we pass the guy who I can
only see his feet. "We are going to meet my uncles Micas and Lucas
and then" He hesitates before finishing his sentence. "My brother"
He says putting me down. "No more trying to run I can hear your
heartbeat so don't bother tip toeing" I huff a house full of werewolves
that all have super senses it is going to be hard as hell to escape this
place and go home.

We walk towards two double doors. "Uncles I bring Morgan Ross"
He says opening the door where two men sit drinking some whisky.
"The famous Morgan Ross?" One says eyeing me with his ocean blue

eyes. "You look just like your mother" The other says catching me off guard. "My mother?" I ask. I never met my mother my aunt raised me. "You Morgan are a legend that will stop this war" Blue eyes says smiling. "Why? I am just human" They both smile "So you think" Why did this have to happen to me! I mean it's cool and all being in a room full of werewolves but not when they can kill you in a second.

"I am Micas by the way" Blue eyes says smiling. "And I am Lucas" The other says. I nod giving a smile back well forcing a smile back. "Cain where is your brother Jaspar?" Lucas asks and at that moment a handsome man comes into the room flashing a smile. "Speak of the devil" The green-eyed man also known as Cain says. "Where is she?" He asks until his eyes land on me. "I'm Jaspar. You must be the legendary Morgan" I nod "So I have been told"

After a few moments where I catch Jaspar staring at me with a smirk. "So, I need information I can't trust you guys I just met you. I need to find out who is killing those teens and why. I also need to know why I am so important to you guys. If you don't give me answers I won't be so easy to tame." I say giving them a stern look. "Feisty I like her" Jasper comment earning a glare from Cain. "Fine will give you answers" Micas says. "You might want to sit down for this" I roll my eyes crossing my arms across my chest leaning against the velvet wall. "We are not the killers the Vampires are they make it look like a wild dog or in this case we killed them but we didn't they just want to scare our kind outside the kingdom. They want to turn our kind against us so they can then kill them and rule the city." I raise an eyebrow "Vampires? Really what is next fairies and unicorns?!" I scoff. "No, they are fake" Lucas says grinning. "Keep going" Morgan commands wanting all the answers spinning in her head to be solved. "We need you. Your mother was the best Luna we could have asked for she was strong, beautiful, and graceful. She let us down the day she had an affair with a Vampire resulting in you the very first hybrid." I was taken back by his words. "Wait so my real father is a vampire and my mother was a Luna? What is a Luna?" I ask "A Luna is a pack leader we have no Luna now but we need one and I think you are the perfect one for the job I mean it's in your blood." I take deep breath. "I don't have any super powers or whatever you call them" I look down at my normal self. "Not yet we haven't done the ritual you usually have when you are a pup but since you were raised with humans then we have to do it now that you are an adult." Lucas says "But for now I am guessing you are overwhelmed with all this so I will send someone to take you to your bedroom" I run my hand through my hair. "I can't believe this I have to go to work in a couple hours!" I say looking out the window as the sun has already risen.

"Here you go" Cain says opening the door for me. "Thank you" I step inside the enormous room. "My room is two doors down if you have any trouble" He informs me before leaving me to gawk at the room before me. This is nothing compared to my apartment back in the city. I snoop around the room opening the closet filled with gorgeous expensive looking dresses. "Those were your mothers" I turn around to see Lucas standing in the doorway. "Was this her room?" I ask already knowing the answer. "Yes, I thought it would suit you. You look just like her" I consider the mirror picturing an older me. "Where you guys close?" I ask earning a small smile from him. "Yes, we were she was my first love I oversaw protecting her while she found her mate; our alpha." I nod touching the soft red silk on the bed. "We are your family now Morgan now more than ever we must stick together to defend ourselves to save humanity and our kind"

After he left I went took a shower this time with no interruptions. I need a plan to contact Sampson that I am all right if the girl did do as I told her then help should have been on its way. Maybe she was too scared and now my boss will think I am a screw up who didn't show up to work today. I can't sleep even though my bones ache and I am tired but I need to do something. I can't just let them control my life. I go over to the closet to pick out some jeans and a t-shirt but all I saw were dresses and skirts. I keep searching until I found two double doors behind a rack of dresses. I opened it to find a walk-in closet filled with more dresses, shoes and pants! I have never been so happy to see a pair of pant. "Finally,"

I walk down the wooden steps wanting to get more information knowing that the one they had given me wasn't the whole truth. Something still didn't make me trust them. I need to find a library or something to research these creatures which now I am one of them. I am not human...I touch my face which feels the same. "Newbie" A voice says I look up and see a tall blonde guy with grey eyes with a giant grin on his face. "That is not my name"

"I know it's the legendary Morgan Ross!" He exclaims. "No, it's just Morgan"

"Okay 'just Morgan' my name is Josh" He says with a playful grin. "So, I heard you are doing the ritual" He says like he didn't just try to kill me with annoyance. "Yes I am. I don't know why this is any of your business" He smiles at my remark. "Feisty. I like you." I smile liking this somewhat of a compliment. "What is the ritual anyways?" I ask hoping he will be an easy way to answers. "You have to stand mostly naked in front of the pack and say some vows then they make you drink something it hurts like a bitch. After that you transform or shift and we all go in and celebrate"

"Mostly naked?"

"Yup'"

"Don't get nervous."

"I don't get nervous"

"You look nervous"

"I do not"

"Do to"

"Do no-okay I feel like a five-year-old doing this with you. I have another question"

"Shoot"

"Do you happen to know if you guys have a library?" He sighs "I thought you were going to say bar but yeah we do but it's off limits only Cain can go in there and he is really moody" I furrow my eyebrows. "Cain moody? I may have just met him like a couple hours ago, but he seems nice" Josh scoffs. "When he is with you but in battle or just anywhere he has a scowl on his face." He says in a low voice. "I feel bad for whoever is going to be his mate"

"What is a mate?" I ask boy do I feel dumb for asking so many questions. "You need to go to werewolf 101 cause you don't know shiz" He grabs my arm dragging me down the halls. "I am going to be your teacher" I roll my eyes at him as he makes me sit down on one of the many couches. "So, lesson one-Mates." Josh begins to say as I try my best not to laugh at this. "A mate is someone you are meant to be with literally the moon goddess chooses a perfect match for you. It is amazing-so I have been told-they say it's more a curse then a gift. You die when they die basically. Unless you get a second chance." I feel like I should be jotting this down from how important he is making all this sound.

"I see you are teaching our upcoming pack member the ropes" Micas says walking into the room. "Morgan the ritual will take place during the next full moon which will be next week" I let out a breath of relief. "So, I can go home?" I say with a small bit of hope. "No" Another voice says I turn and see Cain standing in the door way. "Why not?" I get up from my seat a little annoyed. "Because I said so and what I say I want done gets done you are staying here and that's final" I scoff as he storms out the room. "What's up with him?" I ask Micas who has a grin on his face. "He has been moody all this week ever since he went to the city to look for you" Micas informs me. "That's unusual" I say getting a grin from Josh and Micas. "Morgan come with me I want to show you something" Jaspar says coming into the room. "Okay..." I look back at Josh and Micas as Jaspar takes my hand leading me somewhere. "Where are, we going?" I ask as we go through halls and halls filled with paintings that looks very expensive. "You'll see" He says looking back at me with a kind smile. "I am not good with surprises Jaspar" I say as we go through two glass doors and into a magnificent garden. "Wow this place is beautiful" I gasp as I see all the exotic flowers beautifully arranged. "It is very beautiful" Jaspar says looking at me. "If you ever need to escape mentally you can always come here." It's nice to know that at least one brother is nice to me. "Thank you" I say yawning afterwards. "You must be exhausted with all the news you just got" I nod as I feel my eye begin to droop. "I have never- "I yawn again."-Been so sleepy in my entire life" I stretch not in the mood to walk all the way back. "Let me help you" Jaspar says picking me up bridal style. "What are you doing" I say not trusting this guy I just met. "You are too tired to walk so I'll take you to your room" He says and the rest was all mumbles.

I woke up to loud yelling and stuff being thrown on the ground. I look around the room looking for a weapon any weapon I can take to protect myself. I open the door walking over to the stairs where I see him. Cain but it looks nothing like him his eyes are black his teeth are-I turn away for the first time I am terrified. "Morgan come with me" Josh says making Cain turn swiftly growling the moment Josh's hands landed on me. "Now lock your door and don't come out until morning" I do as he say before Josh goes back down to calm a very angry Cain.

I lay on my bed thinking about the mess I had got myself into. I close my eyes for a minute, when I opened them again Cain was standing in the corner of the room. "What are you doing here?" I ask feeling scared for some reason "You are evil" He sneers. "You are the reason we are all going to be harmed!" He yells attacking me. I close my eyes screaming, but then I am open them in the same spot I was before but Cain was gone. Then I realized it was all a dream. I walk into the bathroom feeling my clothes sticking on me from all the sweat. Once

I finally cooled off I changed into a loose white top and jeans walking bare foot to the garden but then getting an idea. I need to escape I can't live here and fight a war for people I barely met. I look around the house making sure no one is out and about. I open the back door leading to the garden where I climb the tall wall.

I hit the ground on my feet sprinting my way to the only 'secure' place in this damn forest I know the shed. I finally reach it out of breath I look all around as the birds are beginning to die down. I slip through the doors finding a match lighting it before searching for a candle. I find an old dusty candle lighting it up looking for things mostly weapons. I find a stick making it into a spear hiding it by some old tools. I toss the non-threatening tools to one side. What the hell is a shed doing in the middle of the forest any ways? I rummage through all the boxes and other stuff before finding a cute decorated box filled with letters from Catalina to a man named Victor. Curiosity takes over me as I grab the first letter trying not to rip it.

My Dearest Victor,

Oh, how I dread the day we part. Each day I leave you my heart aches I know I am destined to someone it is natural for me, Luca and when I find the right moment I will reject him. We can re-unite my kind with your kind I know they will be angry at first but my love we will go through this together and we will live for eternity as our love will never die. They will hate me for backing out on their new Alpha, Luca but I know that you will make a magnificent leader. I can't wait to see you again. I don't know what excuse to make this time maybe my dress ripped and I need to get it fixed. Or maybe I need a new pair of shoes and I'll send the maids to go fetch them and I'll sneak away where we can meet by the waterfall. I hope no one finds these letters. I have no idea if I should send them to you I do have some important news to tell you I don't know if I should tell you now or wait to tell you in person. They will soon know in a couple months. Oh, I can't wait to tell you! I think I should just tell you now! Oh, my dearest love, I love you so very much and I know you will be as happy as I am to tell you we just made history my lovely Victor we are having a baby and I have a feeling it's a baby girl. I am in love with the name Morgan what do you think. My love she will be the daughter of two loving parents and most importantly two great leaders from two very important kinds. She will be powerful and strong. She will end this war once and for all and maybe if we are lucky we will get to be a happy family. Like I had always wanted a family that I chose to have not that was destined to be. I just want to let you know how much I love you and absolutely adore you but I know you know that.

Forever with you,

Catalina

Chapter three

C HAPTER THREE

After reading many letters from my mother to my father I realize that I am not like them. I am much more and that's why they want me because I am much more than them, much more power-ful than them. I look down at my sore feet cursing myself for not thinking this through...and this feels way too easy, I mean escaping a pack of werewolves just like that without a sweat. I look at the box remembering all the letters she wrote without Victor knowing about her expecting me; the hybrid. She did find her mate; Luca, but she rejected him. I soon realize why the werewolves and vampires hate each other so bad, they were angered by the fact that Luca a very respected man got rejected by the Luna because she was in love with a vampire; my father. I sigh wondering why they didn't accept my father's love for my mother. I never really thought of investigating or asking about my parents, they told me they had died in a car accident when a wild wolf jumped in front of the car. My aunt Matilda never liked talking about them maybe because she didn't want to mention my father was a vampire and my mother was a werewolf. All she told me was that she died of an illness that drove my father mad and he left, found dead somewhere. The two brothers...can I trust them? Can I trust any of them? Fight a war that is not even mine! In a time of war there is betrayal and no one can be trusted, I need to go back to my city where I can fight crime that has nothing to with these...creatures! I must go back but not yet I have to wait a couple days so that the coast can be clear.

A week has past and I have a plan so that I can end this for good because if I leave and go back to my city they will take me from it again. I need to find Victor and tell him I am his daughter and that I am here to stop the war. I also need a shower and I know the perfect place that I saw when I was running. I open the shed doors slowly peeking making sure no wolf creatures are waiting for me. I walk outside a bit blinded by the sun before my eyes readjusts to the change in light. I sigh in relief seeing as no one is near I take a step forward stopping when I hear a crunch, my heart drops to the floor. I close

my eyes getting ready for them to drag me back to the castle.

**

The castle walls looked as if they were watching every move, every

word that passed by them. Jaspar felt as if something was wrong so

he was heading where Morgan was being held. He hadn't seen her in

days, he knocks on the door getting no reply so he opens it finding

that the room is empty. Jaspar growls sniffing her out but her scent

is weak if only he were her mate he would be able to find her. He

goes into the kitchen finding Josh on a stool stuffing his face with a

sandwich, "What?" He says a bit muffled "Where is Morgan?" Jaspar

asks feeling a wave of frustration over power him wanting to tear

the castle apart. "I don't know I haven't seen her since you guys cut

my lecture short" He says going back to eating his sandwich. "Idiot"

Jaspar says once he left the kitchen going to the last person he knows

will be able to find her. Her mate which is also his dear brother whom

he hates so much because he has a higher-ranking pack than his.

Jaspar doesn't even bother to knock opening the door glaring at Cain

who seems calm even though Jaspar knows that he knows Morgan

is gone. "Morgan is gone FYI brother" he says looking around the room. "She is?" Cain asks looking back at his brother "Don't act stupid it doesn't suit you" Jaspar says getting angry at him "Do you know where she is?" He asks wanting to find her so he can get her trust. "No" Cain replies even though he knows exactly where she could be. "You are no help" Jaspar mutters storming out of the room.

**

Morgan stands still knowing that if she runs they will catch her no matter what. "Morgan" She turns around to face Jaspar who is trying to hide his anger hiding it with worry. "I have been looking for you everywhere" He says making Morgan think she is a very important piece that cannot be lost. "Apparently not everywhere" She says giving a pointed look. "We need you Morgan. The future of humanity lies in your hands" He says reaching to touch her but she pulls back. "Why couldn't you guys just breed a hybrid and train them to be like me? Why ruin my life?" She stops talking realizing what she is saying is completely selfish "I am sorry" She says looking at him "I understand why you would be mad I mean you are right! We did ruin your life and by ruining yours we will be saving millions" His eyes light up thinking about the glory of winning the war having Morgan as his wife even though she is his brothers mate but she doesn't need to know that. He can win her over and this is one of the steps he must do to win her over. Morgan scoffs making her way to the castle, Jaspar quickly goes to her side "I am not going to run...can I at least make a phone call Jaspar?" He smiles liking the way his name rolls off her tongue "Of course but only with my supervision" She smiles "Thank you for your kindness" She says thinking of Cain and how he has treated her since they have met. "Can I ask you a question?" Jaspar asks looking at her dirty self "Shoot" She says feeling a little more at ease. "How would you like to have dinner this afternoon with me? After you rest and get clean" Morgan looks down at her clothes that are no longer the color they were at the beginning of the week. "Sure, why not" She says making Jaspar smile already feeling the glory. Morgan looks at the castle feeling uneasy now that she is brought back to the dream and the way Cain acted. "Jaspar? Can I ask you a question?" He nods "What happened to Cain the night before I left?" She asks noticing how his face changed "I don't know he gets angry for no reason...he can be deadly even to those he loves" Jaspar says pretending to be upset for his brothers "anger" issues. "Morgan! You had us all worried" Lucas says showing signs of relief. "I needed time to think...that's all" She says walking past them disappointed that Cain wasn't there.

**

I sit on the bed thinking about the letters in the shed, wanting to find out what happened to my parents. I sigh walking over to the bathroom for a much-needed shower. A knock on the door makes me hurry up no longer taking my time. I quickly dress hanging the towel by the sink opening the door "Hey" I say looking at Jaspar "Hi...I was wondering if you are ready to take the phone call" I smile thinking he forgot about it "Yes please" Jaspar smiles leading the way "So you guys don't have cell phones?" I ask looking at a very old phone "No we have something else that you will later find out" He tells me giving me some room "Are you sure this is going to work" I tell him removing some dust "Yes" He says sitting on one of the many chairs. I dial the number waiting for him to pick up "Hello?" Sampson's voice asks "Sampson! It's me Morgan!" I can already imagine him looking shocked as ever "Morgan? Where the hell have you been, we have been worried sick! Well not me Chief fired you and you have already been replaced" I sigh "Little time to explain...Chief can go to hell I got something way bigger over here" I tell him looking back at Jaspar "Where are you? Do you need backup?" I smile "No. I am fine you won't hear from me for a long time but just know I am safe...anyways take care you can go into my apartment and grab what you like leave my clothes there I'll have someone pick them up" I explain before hanging up. "I'll send someone to grab your things to make you feel more comfortable" I smiles "Thank you Jaspar...I think I am too tired for a dinner now maybe some other time?" He looks sad but I am too tired to deal with interactions "Promise?" He asks smiling "Promise" I tell him walking out the room to see Cain "Cain" I call out but he disappears.

Chapter Four

C hapter four

I walk into the large castle remembering those days where I used to play outside of them hoping that one day I will get to rule inside that castle. It was destiny as Micas once told me when he found out I was to be Luna now that the ones before never had children. I was happy that I would be the next leader to the pack I love and maybe later find the one for me. I never in a million years would think that the person destined to me mine was not to be the one who has my love. I sit on my bed grabbing the journal Micas gave to me telling me that it is where all my secrets can be told without anyone but me can look at. I never understood why Micas was so close to me or why Lucas would look away whenever I talked to him. I begin to write...

Today was a good day, a day like any other day filled with duty and Catalina do this and Catalina what do you think. I never knew that being Luna could be so exhausting! I should have never agreed to this but now there is no turning back I have been Luna for half a century and I need to show them that they can count on me to destroy the Vamps who think they are so classy and powerful just because they have eternal life but they are dark creatures that feed off humans to survive...I have tried human blood but I simply prefer animal because they have a much more balanced diet. I can't even think anymore...I need time to come up with a plan to stop them from taking over I am so close to coming up with one. I need to they are coming to the city and that is never good there are families there and all...I will write soon but for now I keep you locked up behind my closet nobody knows where you are but me. Like Micas said this is where all my secrets can be told and no one will ever know.

Catalina.

***

I am back sweet journal and this time I have great news I met the man that will forever be mine but destiny has a way of giving me what I don't desire like being a Luna I know longer desire it because it is full with a bunch of whiney pups! I have already met my mate and they man I am talking about is not him...his name is Victor and he is...well a Vampire I know several days ago, I was cursing them but now I absolutely adore him...he is nothing of what Lucas or Micas or even the elders have told me. Lucas is my mate but I don't love him not like I love Victor, I don't know if I am ready to love now I don't want to risk my pack getting hurt...I am seeing him again today my maids are going out so I am going to sneak by and meet him by the waterfall. I hear the maids I must go now! Love? Love!

Love,

Catalina

I fix my dress waiting for the maids to come "You" I point at the girl "Take me with you I need to do some errands" I tell her my heart racing "Aren't the guards supposed to come with you?" I shake my head "They are too busy...As your Luna I command you to take me" She bows her head making me smile "Good. Now let's go"

I make my way to the car but the maid stops me "No, we have orders to use the wagon" I force a smile, I never thought I would ride one again. We make a stop along the way and I use that time to hop of the wagon and sneak off to the nearest place we both know.

"Victor"

"Catalina"

The most romantic thing anyone has ever done for me was right in front of me by the water where a cushion was placed, candles were everywhere and a nice warm meal was prepared. "Oh, my love how I missed you" I told him kissing him "I missed you too Catalina" He murmurs smiling down at me "We have little time" He tells me bringing me to the cushion. "I know, I know there will never be enough time"

I don't understand what is happening I thought he understood how I felt and why I am giving up something that can change everything. Am I not entitled to my own happiness? Why does it seem like I am supposed to always put others before me? I know I am their leader, their Luna but they need to understand my needs too. Lucas needs to understand my needs...I need Victor and his opposition is not helping the situation what so ever. I don't understand truly why would the moon goddess send me Lucas when she knows I will encounter Victor and fall madly in love. In times like these I wish I were human...at least they have a choice.

With love,

Catalina

***

I am meeting him again today by the waterfall like always...I am getting very good at making up excuses to leave the castle even though Lucas doesn't like it one bit and gets very angry when I come home smelling a bit different. I am not stupid of course so I rub myself with things from the market surrounding myself in those odors before returning to the castle but he can still tell and he is my mate after all no matter how much I don't want him to be. I must go I will write back soon writing makes me feel relieved.

Catalina

***

He loves me! And he has told his 'pack' or whatever a large group of vampires are called and they are thrilled to be combined with the wolves since they believe it will bring them more power so they can overrule humans but I told them that is not our plan. I plan on living in harmony but they don't like it Victor said getting worried that we won't be together. I hugged him and kissed him making him forget the situation for a while. That was the best night of my entire existence.

Love,

Catalina

***

I rejected Lucas now that I have been with Victor I can't keep pretending to be in love with him because I am not. Lucas isn't powerful like Victor who can kill anything in an instant or as handsome. If I want to be the powerful ruler for my pack I must be with a powerful person and that is Victor not Lucas who takes my every command like the fool, he is being in love with a woman like me.

Even if it was destiny I couldn't see it. I hope he gets a second chance in finding his one and only.

Catalina

I told the pack about my relationship with Victor they were not happy since me being with Victor means Lucas won't be Alpha and they would have to take orders from a red eyed vampire. I can't believe they would do this to me I am their ruler and they shall obey me and my wishes, I will help them I promise I don't know why I must makes this promise maybe it's to myself or maybe it is proof that I intend nothing but good intentions.

Love,

Catalina

***

I am sorry I haven't written in a long time...the situation is complicated now...I don't understand how all of this can happen. I thought he loved me but no he loved my power and status nothing more, nothing less. How could I be so stupid? I had a good man in my hands now that I realized how good Lucas was to me even after I rejected him he still spoke to me somewhat. We have so much to catch up on! I am not living with a human who I trust very much on the run from Victor...Lucas wanted me to leave he told me he will take care of it all and the pack forgave me for my mistake erasing all I did in the past. The vampires are angry and now more that they know I have a hybrid child inside me. Victor wants our daughter but I won't let him have her because he only wants her for power and nothing more. I am now with Matilda for the time being while I recover from my pregnancy Lucas told me before I left that when I come back if he is still alive that he will treat Morgan like his own. Yes, her name is Morgan isn't I lovely! In situations like these she is my hope, my love, my strength.

Forever yours in hiding.

Catalina

***

Morgan is a year old which means I can leave to fix the mess I made...I am sad to leave her even though now I know what my duty is. I am their Luna and it is time I start acting like one...If I don't return I know Morgan will grow to be powerful and courageous the woman I never was even though I am hoping to change that. I leave tears falling down my face but I know it is for the greater good of humanity.

If we meet again,

Catalina

Chapter Five

C hapter five

It has been two days since I was brought back to the castle and nothing has happened. I feel like they are not telling me something. "Morgan" I look up leaving my thoughts behind "Yeah?" Jaspar smiles "Would you like to have dinner with me. You owe me remember" He smiles "Right. Of course, I will" I smile back feeling a bit relaxed to do something new. I walk out of my room and look two doors down where Cain is, I want to go and knock but I stop myself closing the door getting ready.

I walk down the stairs where Jaspar is waiting with a smile for me. "You look amazing" He says "Thank you Jaspar" I smile grabbing the hand he offered. "I reserved the dining room and told everyone it is out of bounds for now" I look down smiling "You shouldn't have gone to all this trouble" He chuckles "I would have done more but with the situation it is best we keep you in the castle" He says making me remember why I am here. "Right...can we not discuss any of this tonight...please, I want to have a normal night dining with a very handsome werewolf" He perks up at my compliment "You think I am handsome?" I smile "Yes now shut up and lead the way I am hungry" He laughs "As you wish" I roll my eyes following him to the dining room. "This is magnificent" I look at the beautifully adorned table with candles all around. "Only the best for you" Jaspar says helping me with my chair "Thank you" I murmur as he sits in the seat next to me since across from me is too far to have a decent conversation. We eat in silence Jaspar stealing a few glances making me stop and smile. "I really like you Morgan" He says making my stomach flutter which hasn't happened since I was in high school. "I like you too Jaspar but aren't we destined to someone? A mate?" He saddens "Yes, but let's hope the moon goddess sees we are a perfect match" I give a small smile hoping she does. "I don't want to do the same thing my mother did to her mate" I tell him seeing a change in him "I know" He stays silent his face looking angry "Are you okay" I ask worried he will lash out like Cain did. Cain, my heart flutters but I make it stop

"I am fine" He says going back to eating his food. I look at him before finishing up, the mood changing and I have a feeling it is because of something I said. My mother rejected Lucas who until now still loves her even though she caused him great pain. "Well, I should be off I have things to do...I would escort you to your room but there is something urgent I must take care of." I smile sadly nodding "Yeah no problem thanks for the lovely dinner" I tell him as he walks out the room but I stay for a while before leaving. I close the door behind me taking a deep breath that gets lost as soon as I see Cain "Cain" I call out "Cain" I call out again louder but I know he can hear me even if I whisper. "Why are you ignoring me?" He turns around "What makes you think I am ignoring you?" My breath hitches as I see those green eyes making me think back to the first time I met him. "Well, I never see you and when I do you seem to disappear" He looks at me his green eyes glimmering "I am busy Morgan preparing and training. You see there are these scary creatures called vampires that want to kill you and this whole pack, I have to make sure you don't get killed" I roll my eyes "I can handle it" He scoffs "No you think you can but this isn't something you can just handcuff they are deadly" He says making me frown "Are you going to train me? Once I am turned" I ask hoping he says yes. "I don't know if my brother would like that"

I look at his now angry face "And why would your brother not like that?" I ask tempting him "He obviously has an interest in you" I bite my lip "I don't know he seemed off when I mentioned mates" I tell him and Cain stiffens "He had the same reaction as you did" Cain looks shocked "Is this like a sibling thing?" I ask smiling "No, where are you off to now?" Cain asks "My room why?" He shrugs "No particular reason" He says his green eyes looking confused "Cain!" Someone yells "We need you now! There has been an attack" Cain runs behind the guy and I also follow.

It was everywhere...blood. I have never seen so much blood but it seems like Cain didn't mind he quickly went to the guys standing near the forest. There was also a young girl with raven hair but that wasn't what brought my attention to her it was the fact that she had blood all over her and a heart in her hand. "Morgan this is Adeline, my cousin" Cain says "It is nice to meet you Morgan" Adeline says bowing her head a bit "You too Adeline" I walk over to the two bodies "One's human" The guy that called us said "Why would they kill a human?" I ask looking at the body "To get us on edge of course" He says poking it with a stick "You should head inside they could come back" Cain says "I am going to clear the area" I nod "I'll go with you" I offer "Dressed like that, it is best if you stay" I look down at my elegant dress I forgot I was wearing. "Fine" I mutter following the other people inside "And Adeline please take a shower and leave the heart with the doctor" Adeline smiles wiping some blood off "Sure thing" I watch Cain leave shifting reminding me of the first time I met him.

Jaspar was waiting for me at the door a worried look on his face "Morgan are you okay?" He asks I nod not in the mood to talking to him. "Morgan we need to talk about the ritual" I stop "Let me change out of this" I say not waiting for his answer.

I walk into the kitchen and grab an apple hoping to distract mysel f...It is 11:04 now and I am not sure if I should be afraid or excited that I am finally going to be reborn into my true form. Maybe this will help somehow safe humanity, Micas and Lucas think so...heck the whole pack thinks so. "Morgan follow me" Jaspar says catching me off guard "It's time isn't it?" He nods "But we have to make preparations" He says holding my hand trying to calm me. "Why can't we do it tomorrow?" I ask not feeling like today was the best time to turn into a hybrid. "We technically are" Cain says stepping inside the room "Right how was the search did you find anything?" I ask remembering the attack but who could forget an attack like that?

"No, but that was a wakeup call we need to do the ritual so you can get the proper training" He says giving me a stern look while Jaspar looks beyond annoyed. "You okay Jas?" I ask touching his arm hoping to get a reaction from Cain for some reason I want him to notice me for not just the girl that is the key to peace but more. "Yeah, I'm fine Morgan" He says giving me a smile "Okay let us begin with the basics" Lucas said entering the room alongside Micas.

It is now 11:55, Jaspar took me to this cabin outside the castle in the middle of nowhere that is where I am supposed to get dressed in a black and bathe in some oils. "Adeline" I smile letting her come in "I brought the oils...Cain told me to help you...well he ordered me but I am always happy to help our new Luna" I smile again but as she said those words I felt a little bit of worry creep inside of me. "Thank you, it is much appreciated" She smiles back filling the tub with the oils. "Now get undressed so you can bathe"

Chapter six

Chapter six

It was almost time, everyone was getting ready for what is to come. She sits by the window waiting for them to come get her. "Morgan it's time" Lucas says looking like a proud father. "I-." She starts but can seem to get the words out of her lips. She is filled with an emotion she can't even explain "It's the oils Morgan" Lucas says offering his hand to help her, she takes it not finding the words to say thank you. "You'll find your voice it is just gone for a moment your body is adjusting" He says as they walk along a path dimmed by candles. "Remember how I told you that you might find your mate tonight?" Morgan nods "I just want you to be careful...I don't want you to get hurt" He says remembering the night he was rejected for a vampire that ended up hurting them all in the end. "Thank you" Morgan says finding her voice giving him a small smile knowing what he must have gone through all because her mother fell in love with someone else. "I loved your mother" He says as they get closer "I know...I cans see it in your eyes" He stops her "Morgan" He says making her face him "When I knew your mother was having you I didn't care that she went off with someone else, I just knew that I was going to love you like the father I will never be" A tear slips down his cheek, Morgan wipes the tear "Thank you Lucas, I don't understand my mother's actions but if it weren't for her mistakes I wouldn't be here" She says looking ahead knowing that what is up ahead will change everything.

The water glistened with the moon making the night seem more perfect than ever, the pack sat quietly waiting for the night to begin. Jaspar smiles at Morgan who smiles back, he knows that they aren't mates but it is not always about destiny. His brother can't take her away from him so he warned him not to be in contact with her from now on or else there will be serious consequences. Morgan stepped into the water barefooted feeling the cold water against her vulnerable skin. Micas makes a symbol on the ground giving Morgan the blade. She looks at it holding it firmly before cutting her palm letting the blood drip on the symbol. Lucas grabs the blade from her wiping it with a piece of red cloth "Let the new era begin" Morgan says her eyes turning black, she looks at her hand that no longer has the cut. "I am going to enjoy this" She says smiling at Lucas then at Jaspar.

Jaspar smiles back but then disappears within the crowd being pulled back by Micas "I need to take you somewhere" He says looking around making sure no one is looking at them "Right now? We have to celebrate" Jaspar says confused but follows Micas who growls at him. They walk into the darker side of the woods "Trust me" Micas says before someone hits Jaspar in the back of the head making him go unconscious.

"Have you seen Jaspar?" Morgan asks Josh "Not since he gave you that flirty smile" Morgan scoffs rolling her eyes "He is not my mate so we can't have anything" She says "Sadly you two would make cute babies but he would be a terrible Alpha" He says relaxing on the couch "Why would he make a terrible Alpha?" Morgan asks sitting next to him while the rest of the pack celebrated a new time and the end of vampires. "Well, in my time of knowing him he seems like the wicked brother" Josh says remembering how he used to bring Cain down and make him look bad. "Oh, c'mon that sounds absurd Cain is the wicked brother he didn't even show up" Morgan says looking

around hoping to see one of the brothers but they weren't there.

"He's awake" A woman says sharpening a knife "Micas, what is going

on?" Jaspar looks around what looks like a cave his vision blurred.

"You will find out soon in enough, for now try to relax please" Micas

looks at the woman giving her a nod. She walks over to Jaspar a needle

in her hand, Jaspar quickly begins to move trying to escape but he

can't the injection making him go dark once again.

Cain pants his body drenched in sweat, the punching bags on the

floor looking more exhausted than he is. He can't stop thinking

about Morgan and he knows that if his brother found out he even

thought about speaking to her he will hunt him down. Cain knows

he can kill his brother but Jaspar knows Cain is not capable of spilling

his brothers blood no matter how cruel he is. Cain will forever live in

agony hiding.

He takes another jab at the punching bag setting it up again, getting

lost in the sound of his punches that help deafen the laughter outside

the gym walls. "Cain? Why aren't you celebrating we need you ener-

gized for when they come again" Lucas says watching him continue

to hit the bag "Are you angry at your brother again?" He asks making

Cain growl with anger the punches getting stronger "What did he do this time" Cain stops wiping sweat off his brow "What did he not do this time" He says drinking from his water "Has it to do with a certain someone" Lucas asks having a feeling that Cain might potentially be Morgan's mate. "Morgan? No." He states firmly but never meets his eyes "Then go, forget about your brother for a minute and have fun" He says hoping he can get through to him "Why should I have fun when they are still out there? We should be training not celebrating" He says his brows furrowed in anger. "We can train all you want but for right now go party or take a nap" Lucas says not wanting Cain to pass out in the middle of a fight. "I am not three years old anymore Lucas" Cain says sitting on the bench feeling tired but not wanting sleep to win him over. "Cain, we both know you have been following unhealthy patterns it is time you put your health first and killing second" Cain chuckles "Fine if it'll make you get off my back." Lucas smiles watching Cain leave the room before punching the bag making it fly across the room. "Whew" He shakes his hand going back to the party a smile on his face.

"How are you feeling?" Micas asks lifting Jaspar's chin up making sure he is still healthy enough to live "Oh. Great!" He replies sarcastically "I bet if it were Cain in this situation he would already be out of those chains" Micas says trying to trigger him. "Well I am not like Cain I have something more than him" Jaspar says making Micas smile in victory "No you are not and that is why we chose you" Micas moves out of the way the dark shadow behind him getting closer until Jaspar is facing a tall red eyed man. "Welcome" He says giving a wicked grin "What are you doing working with a vampire" Jaspar says squirming under the evil eyes. "gaining power duh." Micas says rolling his eyes "and you Jaspar? Are you willing to work with a vampire?" Victor asks mocking him "What will I get in return?" Jaspar asks looking back at Micas who just nods. "Morgan of course. Rose will help you win her love" Jaspar scoffs "Have fun trying to make her love me when her mate is...Cain" He says tightening his face in anger "Like I said Rose will help you" Rose gets up showing Jaspar a bottle filled with a black liquid "This will shut down her instincts to go with Cain and this" She holds up another filled with clear liquid "Will make her go to you, you must drink it too...Not the black one though" she says giving a smile to Victor when she notices Jaspar slowly caving in. "What do you get out of it?" Jaspar asks "Morgan. You will be bringing her to me so we can have a father daughter talk" Jaspar stops to think "That's all you have been killing just to have a talk?" Victor smiles "Yes now if you can be a good doggy and not say a word to anyone you can only trust Micas" He says his face forming a scowl. "Okay. I'm in" Jaspar says even though he feels uneasy on the inside but he doesn't care as long as he has another thing his brother wants. "Oh, honey you didn't have a choice" Rose says making him open his mouth pouring the clear liquid down his throat.

"I am getting worried I haven't seen Micas, Lucas, Jaspar or Cain" Morgan says furiously walking around the room. "What if there was another attack?" She begins to worry "Relax Morgan they can handle it and besides you have your new vamp slash werewolf senses" Josh says making her sit down "Adeline have you seen your cousins" Adeline stops what she was doing noticing how worried Morgan looks "No." She says also getting worried "We don't need to make the others worried try to stay calm" Josh says noticing how the rest of the pack is starting to look at them. Morgan smiles "I am so happy to be a part of this pack" She says but a girl scoffs "You are the whole reason this pack is in danger freak" Josh stands up "You are just jealous Natalia; the real Luna is here we don't need you playing pretend anymore" He says making her shut up. "Don't come crying to me babe when everyone is dead" Natalia says giving a wicked smile before leaving the room. "Who was she?" Morgan asks after a couple seconds of silent. "A wannabe Luna who had a thing with Jaspar to get back at

Cain for not loving her" Adeline says not enjoying the fact she is still breathing. "really?!" Josh says "I thought she actually loved Jaspar" Adeline makes a face "She only loves herself" She says "Well the night come more interesting" Morgan says smelling something familiar. "Jaspar" She says walking outside the room "Jaspar where have you been?" Morgan asks "I see you have been putting your nose to use" She smiles "Seriously I was worried" she says making him smile. "I went to the city and bought you your favorite coffee" He says handing her the coffee that will change everything. "How do you know this is my favorite!" She asks excited to have something that she used drink when she was normal. "I'm Jaspar I know everything" She rolls her eyes taking a sip "Taste a little different, it's probably because I haven't had one in so long" Jaspar nods feeling relieved that the first step has been completed she will no longer feel a thing for Cain.

Chapter Seven

✱ **Sorry it is italicized but this is the only way I can get the whole thing without parts of it deleting...weird I know anyhow enjoy!***

Chapter seven

I woke up feeling like I can do anything "Feeling better today" Lucas asks coming out of the bathroom "Yes thank you" I say watching as he puts the herbs he has been using to help ease the pain away. "I think it is time for you to train"

Tightening my ponytail, I walk into the gym that I never knew existed but a month ago, I didn't know werewolves existed and here they are. "Jaspar" I say walking over to him "Hey Morgan" He says touching my shoulder making my body tingle. "No way" He says his eyes sparkling making me giggle for the first time in a long time "You thinking what I'm thinking?" I nod as he pulls me for a hug "I knew it" He says making me forget Cain and everything else because I no longer feel weird when I think of him. "Mine" Jaspar says kissing me "Yours" I reply even though I feel an unexplainable hole inside of me. "I found my mate!" Jaspar shouts making everyone in the room cheer. "We will celebrate after I kick your butt" I roll my eyes smiling "Bet" I reply getting ready to beat him.

I huff accepting defeat as I once again fall on the floor, "I am the one with more super strength why am I failing" Jaspar smiles chuckling "Babe, you need to use your super strengths" I bite my lip "Last try" I say "Fine" He says. After a couple minutes of fighting he finally falls on the floor pulling me down with him "Guess we both lost" I roll my eyes breathing heavily closing my eyes for a second. "I need a shower" I mutter "Me too" Jaspar says shoving my shoulder "Nice try" I tell him getting up to wipe my sweat with a towel. "Bummer" He mutters smiling at me.

***

Natalia sits outside the garden in one of the chairs replaying it in her head over and over again. "Natalia?" Adeline asks seeing as she looks like something terrible happened to her. Natalia looks up wiping the tears off her face. "I found my mate" She says sniffling but at the same time she laughs "Wow. Isn't that great?" Adeline says sitting next to her "Not when he is a jerk." She mutters looking over at Micas who gives her a smirk putting a finger to his lips. "Who is it? Cain? Josh?" She asks looking over to where Natalia was staring but Micas was gone. "No. I am not ready to tell if that's okay" Adeline nods "I am sorry about Cain I really thought he was sick, I guess he just needed a nap" Adeline nods "Apology accepted" Natalia smiles "I have to go, it was nice talking to you" Natalia says getting a mind link from Micas. Meet me now.

"What took you so long love?" Micas asks caressing her cheek "I was finishing up a conversation" She replies getting closer to him to feel the spark "Why must it be you" She says barely above a whisper "I am thinking the same thing" He replies their lips barely touching "I must reject you" She says stepping away from him "What?!" He yells getting angry "This is not healthy I can't be in another unhealthy relationship" Micas face softens "Love, I really love you and I do not want anything bad to happen to you it is best with what is going to happen in the next couple of weeks." He steps closer to her "Please don't reject me" She smiles kissing him softly "I won't" He smiles pulling her closer to him.

The room was dark, everything was misplaced making it look like there was another attack but there wasn't. Cain was hunched over a chair breathing heavily his heart was weakening as the days go by. No one but Natalia has noticed it gave him hope but then she disappeared to go with her newly found mate; Micas. He knew something was wrong but couldn't figure it out, his hands were shaky so were his legs. Cain couldn't walk, he was too weak to walk. No one will notice his health until he is dead. "Morgan..." He whimpers crawling to the door but stops himself short his heart pounding against his chest. "L-" His eye lips begin to feel heavy until he finally gives in and closes them, his breathing getting slower and slower.

***

I watch the children playing outside as I sit on the balcony. I sigh walking over to my closet looking at all of my mother's clothes hoping to find something that can tie me to her, that can show me how she was before she died. I kick the wall, I kick it again hearing the hollow sound bringing me quick to my knees to open it. I slowly open it putting the loose piece of wall out of my way reaching into the darkness feeling a journal. The letter C was imprinted in gold "Catalina" I murmur opening the journal to begin reading page one.

I close the journal tears brimming my eyes. She never really wanted to be Luna she just wanted the luxury not the duty. I was beginning to see her as my role model but not anymore not after I read how she chose love over keeping the little peace these creatures had. "Morgan" I look up smiling when I see Jaspar. "Hey you" I get up putting the journal facing down so he won't see the letter. "What were you reading?" He asks eyeing the journal "Oh some old thing I found" I say trying to brush it away. "Really? It looks like a journal Catalina had" He says giving me a look that says he knows it all "How do you know?" I ask grabbing the journal protectively "Micas gave it to her and Micas is the second person I am with the most" I raise a brow "Who is the first?" I ask not letting go of the journal as he comes closer. "You of course" I smile "Better be" I say while he caresses my cheek "You look like you've been crying" I shake my head "No I was about to but I don't want to cry for someone like her" He takes the journal from my hands tossing it on the bed "Let's go out, to take your mind off things" I smile "Like out, out of the castle?" I ask hoping he will take me to the city "I think I can make the work" I hug him kissing him softly on the lips "Thank you!" He smiles hugging me back bringing the unforgettable spark between us also conjuring up the hole inside of me. "What's wrong?" He asks holding my hand when he looks at me I snap out of it "Nothing." And I wasn't lying nothing was happening to me, I don't feel the spark anymore.

***

Natalia sat on the plush chair waiting for Micas to finish solving the packs problems. "What does Lucas do?" Natalia asks leaning forward trying to not to bore herself to death "He does the same we split the work in half but right now his priority is gaining Morgan's trust so she can stay" Natalia grimaces "I hope she leaves" Micas smiles "She will if things go according to plan" He says looking at a very confused Natalia "Very soon my love...very soon" He repeats smiling at the wave of power he is going to receive. "Are you almost done babe I am getting bored" She replies smiling at him even though he can tell she is annoyed. "Almost" He mumbles getting back to the paperwork. "Well I am going for a walk while you finish" Natalia says giving Micas a quick kiss on the cheek before leaving.

She makes her way to Morgan's room but instead goes into Cain's wanting to see how he has been. "Cain?" She knocks on the door but it opens slowly "Cain?" she asks again walking slowly inside "O' my-MICAS!" She screams running out of the room after seeing a pale motionless body on the floor. Natalia keeps running tears in her eyes "Woah there" Micas says catching her by surprise "Cain" She looks at Micas with a scared look in her eyes. "We have to help him!" She yells pulling Micas but he doesn't move "It's for the best, Natalia that he is gone" He tells her giving her a smile trying to comfort her. "Cain dying is for the best of what Micas?!" She screams moving away from him but he pulls her close again. "If we want everything to go according to plan we have to take these measures even if it means hurting one of our own" He wipes away her tears "We have to stick together if we want to survive Natalia because something big is coming and fast" He whispers in her ear. Natalia finally calms down waiting for Micas to let his guard down she can go and think about the choice she must make.

***

I lay on my bed remembering the girl I used to be before I was brought here, back in the city. The only friend I had was Sampson and he was my partner so we kind of had to be friends if we wanted to get anything done. I never liked someone the way I like Jaspar, well only in high school but that is every teenage girl. Never went out, always working my butt off going home to an empty apartment with no one. I was alone and now that I have so many people around me I am starting to finally see that this is what I am supposed to do. I am supposed to be with Jaspar and become the Luna of this pack that will bring down my father. "You look worried" I jump looking at Adeline who smiles "You scared me" I say putting a hand over my heart "Please" She says rolling her eyes "Why were you so worried?" I sigh making room for her on my bed "I just have a bad feeling about it all" I bite my lip trying to figure it out. "I am trying to figure out but I can't I need more information but no one is willing to give me any" Adeline sighs "Well have you tried asking Cain? I know you guys aren't super friendly but if you really want answers he is the person to go to" I furrow my brow clenching my teeth "I don't I haven't even seen him all this week!" I say looking at Adeline who gets serious "Wait you haven't seen him either?" She asks I shake my head "No" She stands up beginning to get nervous "No one has seen him I thought at least one person would see him and you were my last hope" She says running a hand through her hair. "We need to go find him" I look at her sadly "I can't Adeline, I have plans with Jaspar and I don't think he will like me ditching him to find his brother who

for all we know can be hiding from us." I tell her and she nods "I get

it. I'll find him myself." She says leaving the room.

Chapter Eight

Micas looks at the dim room watching Cain dying before his eyes "It had to be done, Son" He says looking at the boy he saw grow up he was always more found of Cain but preferred Jaspar who did as he was told. The perfect soldier Cain would call him when they would argue. He never told them, he didn't want things to change. Micas crouches down touching Cain's cold pale face "Find peace" He whispered before finishing up what he came to do. He grabs different herbs making a circle around Cain opening the door so the wicked witch Rose could come in and do the spell. "No one will see him, right?" He asks looking down at his son "I promise you nothing can overpower my spells" Rose says opening her spell book. "Relax Micas, If Victor promised us power, power is what we will get" She reassures him, he nods making her relax.

"Micas, I love you." Maria says her forehead drenched in sweat "I love you too, that is why I am not letting you go" He kisses her softly watching as she slowly begins to close her eyes "No. Don't leave me" He cries as the doctors' rush in to help her stay awake. "I can't-I can't lose you" He sobs pulled away by Lucas who looks at him with sad eyes. The room goes silent the only thing you could hear were Cain and Jaspar crying "We ate very sorry Alpha Micas" the doctor said bowing his head "Would you like to see your son's?" The nurse asks hoping the mention of his newborns would make him better. "No. Those are monsters! They killed her!" He screamed but stops once Lucas calmed him down. "I will stand with you until the end" Lucas says knowing very well the pack has lost an Alpha.

"We will stand together and rule while we find an excellent Luna" Lucas says watching as Micas stared down at the crib "Yes." He replied not bothering to look at him. "I will not be a father to them. I am their uncle and I will shape them so they can be great soldiers" He says before leaving the room.

"All done, they will see him but it will just be part of their imagination" Rose explains beginning to put her things away "Make sure no one sees you" Micas says his eyes never leaving the spot where Cain was. "I know what I am doing Micas" Rose says rolling her eyes before walking out the room. "Better" Micas mutters leaving the room as well.

I walk outside smiling as I see Jaspar standing by a black car "Ready to go?" He asks "Yes" I reply happy to be out of the castle and back to the city I once protected. "You are itching to see the city, aren't you?" He asks making me smile "Aren't you?" I ask turning up the radio. "I love the City but I prefer the comfort of my castle" I roll my eyes "This all seems like a dream" I say looking out the window "It feels like one to" He adds interlocking his hand with mine keeping his eyes on the road "Life is crazy, I mean I am a hybrid living in a castle full of werewolves and my father is a vampire that is evil" I say realizing how crazy it all sounds. "That was a great summary babe" Jaspar says humming to the music. "I don't know if I am ready" I tell him running a hand through my hair. "Ready for what?" Jaspar asks stopping the car so he can look at me "I don't know to fight, I mean I protected people for a living...until I got fired but I don't know if I want to" I say thinking back to how my mother felt. "I've done things...I've done things that I regret and I have also not done things and those are the ones I regret the most" He tells me squeezing my hand "I am your mate and I will stay with you forever" He says meeting my eyes but somehow it doesn't make me feel better.

Natalia sits outside on the grass on the look-out for anyone who is looking for Cain. "Natalia!" Adeline yells running towards her "Have you seen Cain?" She asks making her smile "Yes! He went out for a run... he is training to hard I tell him but since I'm not Morgan he doesn't listen to me" She says shrugging hoping the spell will work "Really?" She asks "Yes girl! You should relax before the bloodshed begins" Natalia says making it dramatic "There is nowhere to go" Adeline says "Follow me! I know the perfect place" Natalia smiles turning around Adeline following close behind.

"Wow when did you find this place?" Adeline asks amazed by the waterfall "Micas showed it to me it was like our first official date. He was super cute and sweet telling me how he hasn't done anything for a woman for a long time" Natalia says genuinely smiling "Yes I remember my uncle Lucas told me about his last love" Adeline says "What was her name?" Natalia asks not liking the thought of Micas with someone else "Maria they weren't really mates so the moon goddess punished them" Adeline says saddened by the story "She died and well he was living wishing he could be with her that made him loose his title as Alpha giving it to Catalina and well now we are here" Adeline says sitting beside Natalia "So does that make me your aunt?" She asks "I guess so" Adeline replies still thinking about the story. "Maria got what she deserved" Natalia said huffing "She didn't deserve to die" Adeline says watching the water fall.

"I forgot how much I loved the city" I say walking around downtown smiling at everything. "I am sorry things turned out the way they did" Jaspar says holding my hand "You can't mess with destiny" I say laughing but Jaspar turns serious "I guess you can't" He replies in a whisper. "Are you okay" I ask touching his shoulder making him flinch "Yes, like you said life is crazy and it's about to get even crazier" I nod leaning my head on my shoulder. "I'm scarred Jaspar...I don't want to lose any of you guys" I admit my voice becoming shaky, Jaspar wraps his arms around me not saying a word making me feel uneasy.

Chapter Nine

Chapter Nine

"Brother I feel like we haven't spoken in a while" Micas says stepping inside the room "You seem to disappear on me Micas how am I supposed to find if I don't know where you go anymore" Lucas says handing Micas some papers "Here is the strategies the men have been using" Micas smiles "Perfect, this is what I have been waiting for" Lucas takes the papers back putting them away. "You seem distant brother..." Micas sighs checking his pocket where a dagger lies "Yes well I have some bad news" Micas says before giving a grin. "What is it?" Lucas asks ignoring the grin that made his worry grow. "Well you see, I have been noticing something strange in Morgan. Do you think she is keeping contact with her father?" Micas asks even though he knows the answer to all the question he is about to ask. "I don't know" Lucas says questioning his trust. "We must keep an eye on her, where is she now?" He asks "I don't know"

I sit on the bench enjoying the view, the people walking around without a care in the world. They are human and once upon a time I also thought I was human. "You okay?" Jaspar asks sitting next to me "Yeah I am just thinking about stuff" I tell him wishing I could enjoy this moment alone. I need to talk to someone that could help me figure this whole thing out. Maybe I could ask Josh if he could teach me more of the basics since the library is off limits since its Cain's...I wonder where he is...I can't stop thinking about him but I push him at the very back of my thoughts because I am with Jaspar and he is my mate. "You seem really quiet...do you want to go back?" He asks putting his arm around my shoulder "We should buy some food and have picnic" I say wanting to be away from here, it is only making me moody "I know the perfect place a bit far from the castle and trust me it is beautiful" He says smiling at me "Perfect" I tell him getting up from my seat.

"Morgan" Jaspar says his eyes on the road "When all of this is over..
.you will officially be crowned Luna which will bring many respon-
sibilities-." I cut him off getting annoyed "I know Jaspar, I have been

told this many times! I just wish things weren't like this...sometimes I just want to be normal, I miss my job" I say lowering my voice trying to calm myself down "I'm sorry things turned out the way they were but you just have to suck it up" Jaspar says sounding a bit annoyed himself "I'm not very hungry anymore maybe we should just go back to the castle..." He nods "Let's leave the picnic for another day when vampires aren't on the hunt for our heads" he says giving a quick smile "I agree" I say but pause when I hear a scream "Stop the car!" I yell making him swerve until we finally stopped. "Someone is in danger"

Adeline looks out into the water "I don't understand what is going on Natalia, all I know is that when the time comes to fight I will be ready to do so alongside Morgan my Luna" Natalia stands behind her "I wish that to happen but with certain threats I doubt it" She replies giving a smile "What do you mean?" Adeline says facing her now "Well, I have been spending a lot of time with Micas, obviously since he is my mate but he has been telling me things and well I want to help him" Adeline looks at Natalia confused "Of course we have to stick together" Adeline says not liking the way she was looking at her "You were the only friend I actually had here and when things got bad you changed but now we are back together..." Natalia took a step forward making Adeline take a step back. "I know things have been hard with us but now you found your mate and well I'm still looking" Natalia smiles pushing a strand of hair behind her ear "I know and you might never find them unless you survive" Adeline furrowed her brows confused "Survive what?" She asks feeling worried but she wasn't scared. "This." Natalia says pushing her off the edge watching her scream as she falls into the water. "Two down, one more to go" She smirks leaving Adeline for dead.

Jaspar and Morgan both run towards the water fall "I think that's Adeline!" Morgan yells getting ready to jump to go save her but Jaspar was a step ahead diving in to save his cousin. Morgan paces around until she remembers this was the place her mother used to meet with Victor. "She's wet but safe" Jaspar says holding a shivering Adeline "I think Victor had something to do with this" Morgan says making Jaspar serious "Why would he try to hurt Adeline?" He asks "It wasn't Victor unless Natalia works for him" Adeline says in between shivers "Let's take you home" Morgan says wanting to ask more about what happened later when Jaspar is not around.

He rushes quickly forgetting about the plan. The bigger picture that Micas has to keep reminding him about. Jaspar finds Micas alone facing his own problems with his brother who is now gone to find answers of his own. "You never told me Adeline would be put in danger!" Jaspar yells infuriated "My brother is one thing but Adeline? Uncle how can you do this to family?!" Jaspar shouts not realizing the hypocrisy in his words. "I could ask you the same thing dear nephew but I mind my own business" Micas says sitting comfortably on the red velvet couch, a glass of whiskey in his hand. "Why Adeline though? I don't get it...I understand Cain he is a threat because he is Morgan's true mate...no matter how much that pains me" Micas sighs "I don't know...I told Natalia to keep an eye out and get rid of any one who was a threat so maybe..." Jaspar silences him "What will we do?" he asks even though he knows the answer cracking a piece of his cold heart. "What we have to do..." Micas replies not wanting to feel the pain of seeing his son that way making him seem almost human.

Natalia looks into the mirror smiling back at her reflection "What have you done?" Micas almost yells but tries to keep his calm. Natalia frowns turning to look at him "What we had to do. She was a threat questioning everything and then she- never mind" Natalia says stopping herself from becoming the jealous mate. "If you wanted to kill you have to do a better job at that" Micas says trying to figure out a plan to make sure Adeline doesn't spill everything. "I did!" Natalia yells defending herself "No you didn't, she is still alive. Morgan and Jaspar found her" Natalia smiles "But Jaspar is on our side" Micas rolls his eyes "Yes but Morgan isn't" Natalia sighs "It's my problem honey, I'll take care of it!" She says giving him a quick kiss ready to leave the room but he pulls her back "Make it happen for real this time" Natalia smiles wickedly "I will" she says before leaving the room.

Micas walks the empty halls looking for his brother so that he can distract him "Brother I don't think we finished our previous conversation" Micas says making himself comfortable "I think we had finished" Lucas says putting some papers away before looking up at his brother. "I have some information..." Micas says giving a grin "Important or your everyday gossip Micas because being on the brink of war is not giving me the joy of anything" Micas rolls his eyes yawning "You are such a bore brother did I ever tell you that?" Lucas scoffs "I have a serious question to ask if you don't want to listen to my information" Micas becomes serious "How did you not die when Catalina died." Lucas stiffens taking a deep breath "Why do you need to know this?" Micas shrugs innocently thinking about killing his very own brother. "For future reference" Lucas thinks for a while left speechless as he relives his grief.

Lucas walks into the castle his shirt splattered with blood. "We finallyfought them off sir" one of the men said making Lucas smile "We did didn't we?"his smile fades when he saw one of the trained nurses with a tear stained facelooking at him for help. "I have to go!" Lucas says running towards her "Whathappened" He asks not wanting to know what happened but he also doesn't want tobe left thinking the worst. "Our Luna-" She sobs wiping away her tears makingLucas panic leaving her to find his love even if she loved another man he stillloved her. "Catalina!" He yelled looking in each of the rooms his heart racing."Catalina!" He stops when he saw Micas standing in front of her room "Micaswhere is she?" Micas turns and looks at him his eyes filled with grief "gone."Lucas stops himself from lashing out at him for who knows what reason. Hisworld was spinning he didn't know what to do then he remembered the pain hethough was a cut was really his heart telling him that Catalina was dead. "No.No. No." Lucas mumbled looking at Micas "I am sorry brother. I truly am"

"Lucas?" Micas calls out bringing him back to reality "I am sorry but I don't know how to answer that question brother...the moon goddess gave me a second chance in life I guess" Micas sighs not liking the response he got from him. "I am sorry for making you relive that day" Micas says sincerely remembering the reason his brothers world was turned upside down. "It just makes you realize how someone you love can bring you so much pain" Lucas looks down at his hands while Micas gets ready to kill his brother that was weakened by the memory of his beloved Catalina. "Lucas I know this is all very hard but there is no other way to survive this war" Micas takes the dagger out. Lucas finally realized what his brother was implying "Micas...why?" Micas smiles "Well...Victor promised me something I just couldn't turn away and I know how much you love this pack but they aren't strong like the vampires. One bite and we can die." Lucas shakes his head "This is unbelievable! How can you do this to me, to our pack, to our family for crying out loud?" Micas laughs "This isn't me any more I don't like being second in command. I am tired Lucas and this is my way out" His desperation for something more made Lucas feel almost bad for his brother but then he remembers why he is here. "Killing me is your way out?" Mica sighs "I wish it weren't but yes, It is" Lucas sighs as Micas comes closer ready to finish his task. "I am sorry brother" Micas says "No you are not" Lucas replies standing still not caring if he died at this point.

Chapter Ten

Chapter ten

I watch over Adeline who took a warm bath sitting next to the fireplace I lit for her. "I can't believe Natalia would do that" I say wondering how she is connected to everything, what her motive could be. "Honestly I have no idea why she would want to hurt me...we were getting along until I mentioned Micas having someone else." Adeline says looking hurt "I thought she changed" She says playing with the pillow on her lap. "Who was Micas other lover?" I ask hoping this mystery woman can help me understand why Natalia would want Adeline dead. "Her name was Maria all I know was that they were punished by the moon goddess because they weren't mates so she died" She watched me "What's wrong?" I shake my head "Nothing...I just got a bad feeling" I tell her thinking about Jaspar

"Anyways why were you there anyways?" I ask thinking back to my mother's letters "I was looking for Cain when I saw Natalia and I asked her, she said he went for a run getting ready to train the boys" My heart leaps at the mention of Cain but my mind ignores it "Have you seen Cain?" Adeline shakes her head sadly "Morgan...what if she did something to him?" I hold her hand reassuring her "Cain is too strong for that" Adeline smiles "You are right" I smile back at her "I am going to look for Cain even though Jaspar will hate me for it we need him" Adeline smiles hugging me "Thank you!" I hug her back standing up "You sure you are good up here? I could call Josh so he can watch you" I offer but she shakes her head no. "I am good...go find my cousin.."

I walk out making my way to his room hoping he is there so that my mind can be at ease. "Josh!" I call out jogging up to him "Hey Morgan I haven't seen you in forever!" He says looking relieved to see me "I was beginning to worry since I haven't seen Cain all day" I frown "Neither have I" He sighs "I have to go train with the rest of the guys. Take care...seriously because it is dangerous outside" I smile sadly "I know Josh...who's training by the way?" Josh shrugs "I have no idea...maybe Jaspar but he doesn't really know how to fight as well as Cain-Don't tell him!" I laugh "I won't." I watch him leave before making my way to Cain's room.

"Rose."

"Jaspar."

Jaspar watches as she pours different liquids into one container "What is that for?" He asks "For you darling!" Rose responds putting the liquid in a needle "Just in case your little girlfriend gets out of hand" Jaspar smiles "I highly doubt it but I will keep it close" Rose rolls her eyes "Oh c'mon Jaspar we both know you will need it! I've seen how she can get wandering off and getting into detective mode!" She says putting her stuff away "What are you doing in the castle anyways?" Jaspar asks watching her closely "Exploring" She says giving a wicked smile. "Don't get caught" Jaspar warns making her frown "You are just like your father...oops" Rose says forgetting he didn't know Micas was his father. "You knew my father?" Rose sighs "No, I know your father now don't go all crazy but Micas is your father" Rose says leaving the room before he did something to her. Jaspar sits on the nearest chair before realizing he had to go speak to him.

"Micas please brother" Lucas pleads hoping to buy some time and give some sense to his brother "Begging isn't really your think Lucas" Micas says playing with the dagger. "Jaspar is just like you following orders here and there wanting what he brother has...I know what you are up to Micas" Lucas says hoping this will make Micas tell him what he is planning. "Oh really? Tell me then...do you know Cain is locked away somewhere dying because his mate is too busy with his brother to care...why wouldn't she care you ask? Isn't she his mate? Yes she is but you see I am smarter than any of you and I have a witch on my side creating potions you have never heard of" His eyes light up with passion and rage as he explains to his brother "I want you to see them suffer but I won't give you the luxury of living any longer" He clutches the dagger in his hands getting ready "I hope you live a good life brother even if deep down you are miserable"

Adeline sat on her bed waiting for Morgan to barge into her room with Cain following behind her so she could forget about all her worries and focus on the upcoming war if there even is a war. She walks over to the window opening it no longer bothered by the cold air. "Hey bestie! I thought you were dead." Natalia's voice said making Adeline turn around. "You should try harder next time" Natalia smiles "Oh I will trust me and when I am done with you..."

She chuckles holding to blades one in each hand "You won't know what hit you" Adeline shakes her head getting ready to fight even if it means killing one of her own "Really Natalia weapons, that says something about you" Adeline tsks at a glaring Natalia. "Does my uncle know you are going to kill me?" Adeline says trying to get some leverage "Yes. He ordered me to" Natalia answers a giant smirk on her face "Well then he is as dead as you are going to be" She growls her eyes glowing.

I walk down the empty hall getting a bad vibe. I wish I has something to defend myself, I take a deep breath before grabbing the handle. As I was about to open the door I hear a scream that makes me forget everything "Adeline!" I yell running towards her room. "Jasper!" I yell "Adeline-." I stop and take a deep breath "She is in trouble" I tell him but he seems serious "She can handle herself...Morgan. Micas is my father" I stop myself from running past him "What?" I shake my head remembering Adeline in danger "We can talk later Adeline's in trouble" my heart races as I hear another scream "Jaspar!" I nudge him "I'm sorry" He says before I feel a pinch on my arm.

I wake up in a dark cold room, my eyes look around but my vision is still blurry. "Help" I try to say but nothing comes out. I try to move but I seem to be paralyzed by whatever was in the shot. Adeline could be dead by now and I am who knows where unable to leave. My vision becomes too blurry to see shapes all I see is blobs of color. I begin to hear footsteps and soon a familiar hand is caressing my cheek. Jaspar! I try to lift my head but it is too heavy, "I'm sorry Morgan. It has to be done" He says and I can tell he is looking at me. I try to move, to fight back but I can't making me even more angry. "I know you are probably pissed but it is for your best...you are going to meet your father" my heart jumps for a second scared, I must escape. As the door closes I relax trying to move my body so I can tell Lucas the truth.

I walk out leaving Morgan alone with her thoughts. I know she is probably angry but I am doing this for her own good. "Jaspar! I have been looking everywhere for you!" Josh says sounding annoyed but relieved to see me "Why?" I ask wanting to finish this conversation so that I could have one with my father... "Well you are the one that is supposed to train us since Cain is nowhere to be seen" I sigh thinking about my two options. If I train with them I will know exactly what they will do but if I don't they will be unprepared for the vampires... "Cancel it today, we will meet tomorrow at dawn" I lie because by tomorrow this whole pack will be history.

Chapter Eleven

The room was a mess when Jaspar walked in finding a bloody Adeline and a Dead Natalia. "What have you done?" Jaspar says falling on the floor holding Natalia "What I had to do to not end up like her" Jaspar gets up walking past Natalia's body "You ruined my plan"

1 Hour before

Jaspar walks around the castle trying to figure out what to say to Micas. He still wonders who is mother is...maybe he could ask him that. At this point he doesn't know what to do with his life. Jaspar doesn't realize that what he is doing to the people he cares about. "Jaspar, I heard some screaming coming from Adeline's room" one of the helpers says sounding concern "Just ignore it for now I'll check it out in a bit" Jaspar says not able to look her in the eyes because he knows his cousin is in danger.

He walks over to Morgan lifting her limp head. Her paleness scares Jaspar making him want to inject her so she can be her normal self but he doesn't because he knows what will happen if he does. The potion will be gone when she wakes up and she will no longer go with him but with his brother who is dying as we speak. "I am sorry for what I did to you and Cain but this is less painful than what the vampires have planned...well for the rest of the pack" Jaspar chuckles his dark side re-emerging "I don't want anyone to die but werewol ves...we started killing innocents and well the vampires will stop the killings" If only he knew Morgan was listening closely pitying Jaspar for thinking the vampires are the good guys in this story. "I have come up with a plan though so don't worry about Adeline soon she will join us...I will threaten her to think I am going to kill you unless she joins" He says kissing Morgan's forehead leaving her alone once again.

Adeline looks down at Natalia's body pitying her for being so gullible and falling for the vampire's tricks. "It had to end this way or else you would kill me and the vampires would have the upper hand" She sighs feeling bad for her uncle Micas who will soon feel the pain of losing yet another one of his loves.

"What's taking so long brother? Why not kill me now" Lucas says looking at his brother who takes a step back weakened "Natalia" He whispers falling onto the ground his fist keeping him from falling forward. Lucas uses this advantage to take the dagger "I guess things did not play out the way you wanted them to" He says kicking his brother down "I will not be merciful this time brother" He shouts kicking him in the stomach "Your precious Natalia is dead because of you! She wouldn't be dead if she had a different mate" Micas laughs sounding weak "I did not drag her into this she did herself she wanted to make me happy" He lied trying to conceal the pain inside of him. "We both know nothing will ever make you happy" Lucas walks closer to him placing the dagger on his cheek before cutting him. "Hope you rot in hell brother" Lucas spat kicking him again. "Now that I have you where I want you... I must ask you something" Lucas kneels next to Micas "What exactly happened with Catalina? Don't lie to me" Lucas asks toying with the dagger. "Why do you want to know she is already dead" Micas says earning a punch from Lucas "Don't be an idiot" Micas sighs feeling his body ache.

Present

"You ruined my plan" Jaspar groans looking down at Natalia's body "What plan? The plan where you let your cousin die?" Adeline shouts seeing a darkness in her cousin's eyes "No." Jaspar says trying to figure out how to let Adeline know what is going to happen "What did you get yourself into?" Adeline asks taking a step back but Jaspar takes a step forward making her hit the drawer behind her. "Well you see the vampires are going to kill this whole pack and they have told me to recruit some mutts for them" Jaspar smiles "and well I don't want you to die but if you don't join you and Morgan will both die" Adeline growls "What did you do to Morgan? If you kill her you die too you idiot" Jaspar chuckles "No I won't and Morgan is locked away somewhere in this maze of a castle, but you won't be able to find her in time so I suggest you join me" Adeline smiles back at him. "Fine but you have to keep Morgan alive if you want me to be loyal to you" Jaspar claps his hands "Perfect!" He says walking towards Natalia throwing her limp body over his shoulder as if it were a sack.

As soon as Jaspar leaves Adeline quickly rushes towards the door making sure he didn't lock it. Adeline swings it open running towards the exit but she bumps into someone making her fall back.

"Adeline" Josh says picking her up from the floor "Josh! – wait are you brain washed by Jaspar?" She asked looking into his soft blue eyes "Brainwashed?" He asks looking at her curiously "Cain is dying and we need to find Morgan, reverse the spell, and cure Cain" Adeline says remembering Jaspar's words "No I won't" when she said he will die if Morgan does. "Well we need to act quick if we want to beat Jaspar" Adeline shakes her head "It's not Jaspar we should be worried about...there is someone else"

Jaspar dumps Natalia in the corner making his way to Morgan who looks paler "I am sorry but I promise you everything will be okay...just like how Victor promised us all" He whispers fixing a strand of hair sighing "Why are you destined to be my brothers and not mine" He kisses her cheek before leaving her not knowing she is slowly dying.

Chapter Twelve

Chapter Twelve

Lucas looked down at Micas who slouched like a coward "Cat got your tongue? I asked you a question and I expect it to be answered!" Lucas said holding the dagger near Micas' mouth "Or should I cut your tongue?" Micas smiles looking up at his brother "Wow" He says his smile getting bigger "You really are something else...kill me but that is not going to get you any answers" Lucas groans kicking Micas again making him spit more blood. "Fine you want to know the truth? Okay I'll tell you the fricken' truth" Micas tries to get up making Lucas become defensive "Relax" Micas says putting his hands up walking over to the nearest chair "Story time needs to be comfortable" He says chuckling even though in his eyes there was nothing but sadness and hate.

***

Lucas looks outside the castle as shadows of the vampire begin to appear "Catalina" He says looking back at her with fear "You have to hide...Victor will find you" Catalina looks outside and then at Lucas "He is here for me it would be selfish if I let my men die because of it" She says looking down at her hands "No he is here for the baby" Lucas says "If he finds you and sees you don't have her he will kill you" He shouts not wanting to lose Catalina. "Fine!" She says storming away but Lucas pulls her back "wait for me by the well in an hour" Catalina nods making Lucas smile "Be careful Lucas" She whispers before leaving.

Catalina rushes past Micas who heard everything angry at his brother for not sacrificing her for the greater good of the pack. She is the reason why his best men are dying; the pack shouldn't pay for a decision she made even if she is the Luna. Micas goes back outside preparing to face Victor so he could negotiate.

"Did Catalina send you?" Victor asks his sharp fangs threatening to tear Micas flesh "No. I came here on my own" He says preparing his wolf in case he needs to come out. "Why are you here?" Micas asks,

"For Catalina of course I need to talk to her" Victor says desperately

"Stop killing my men and I will tell you where she is" Micas says

hoping his brother will understand. "Fine" Victor says his eyes flash-

ing red and soon Micas was surrounded by vampires. "Now where is

she?"

***

Lucas stayed quiet for a long time before looking back at Micas "I can't believe you told him where she was!" He yelled grip-

ping the dagger turning his knuckles white. "I had to do what is best

for the pack" He said blood still spilling from his cut lip. "You deserve

to rot in hell" Lucas says stabbing Micas letting him fall on the floor.

"You have no idea what is coming!" Micas yelled hysterically as Lucas

walked out the room. As soon as he shut the door he heard a groan

and then silence. Lucas sighs dropping the bloody dagger on the floor

before roaming the castle engulfed in his own thoughts.

***

Micas walks down the city streets replaying Lucas reaction when news of Catalina's death came to the castle. He no longer cared it was his fault she was dead because he is no longer the kind man he used to be. Micas used to envy his brother because he could be with his mate while his love died leaving him with two sons who don't even know he is there dad. "Sorry" He says bumping into two teenagers before entering the dark alley. "Micas I've been wanting to have a chat with you" A vampire says showing his fangs "What do you want?" Micas says preparing his wolf "I heard you wanted to become one of us" the vamp said snickering "Why would I want to be a dirt bag like you?" Micas growled "I know why you are here..." the vamp says smirking his fangs touching his lip "Victors daughter is here and you want to have her for your own" He says stepping closer to Micas gaining confidence. "Just like you betrayed Catalina you are going to do the same with her daughter? That is cruel even for a monster like you...what would your pack think about it?" The vampire said threatening to tell them so they can turn against him. "If they don't know about it they won't think about it" Micas says ready to rip him to shreds. "For now," the vampire says ready to leave but Micas grabs him by the neck killing him instantly. "Oh-my-gosh!" A scared voice yelled making Micas turn showing his werewolf eyes

"Hector!" Juliet screams as they both stand there in fear watching the man turn into a beast. All that was heard was a scream followed by a chilling growl. It had to be done Micas thinks to himself looking at the bodies wiping blood off his face.

Chapter Thirteen

C hapter Thirteen

I don't know for how long I have been trapped here...I seems like a couple of days. My head aches but my entire body feels numb. I can hear when Jaspar comes in to "check-up" on me little did he know I was slowly becoming weaker because of him. Even if his touch makes my wolf feel better it is not fulling healing the poison in my veins. I don't know if Jaspar knows he is slowly killing me. I hope that when I wake up this nightmare of a life will be over. I can't take it anymore. There is so much...I try to open my eyes my body anxious to see something other than black but it is no use. Even though I can feel someone else's presence I don't know who they are. I can't believe Jaspar got tangled up in this, I hope he pays no matter how much it will hurt my wolf. I try to move again hoping the other person in the room is not a vampire because that would mean Victor would be near.

***

Adeline watched the rain drops slowly glide down the windows as Josh drives them to the city. "You sure we can trust a witch?" Josh asks snapping Adeline back to reality "Yes, she might even know who the witch that poisoned Morgan is" Adeline says as they enter the darker part of the city. "You can stay in the car if you are scared" She says smirking at him "You need me just in case things get violent" He says making her roll her eyes.

They walk inside a small shop full of herbs and enchanted stones. "Vivien Grace" Adeline calls out as Josh walks around the store eyeing everything. "Adeline?" A young women around the age of Morgan comes down from the stairs. Her long black hair pulled up in a high pony-tail making her eyes more cat eyed. "What happened?" She immediately says sensing something was wrong from the look of Adeline's face. "A lot has happened in the last couple of days" Josh says "Follow me" Vivien Grace says before snapping her fingers locking the front door "No interruptions" She says as they make their way to a dim room filled with candles of all shapes and sizes each one a different color. "We are hoping you can reverse a spell" Adeline says hoping the past two days trying to find her are going to be at good use. "What kind of spell" Vivien Grace asks pouring them tea "An unknown witch made a potion that poisoned both my cousin Cain and his mate Morgan...they are dying because they are not together" Adeline takes a sip of the tea hoping it will calm her down "Who is involve I'm sure it was someone from inside the castle" Vivien Grace asks crossing her arms across her chest. "My cousin Jaspar is involved but we don't know who the witch is, all I know is that they are working with vampires." Vivien Grace's eyes quickly look at Adeline's "Rose" She mutters making her hands into fists "She betrayed her coven thinking she was going to obtain more power" Vivian Grace says shaking her head "Instead she became their lap dog doing as told" Adeline looks at her "Can we reverse this?" Vivian Grace opens the black book in front of her "Of course we just need a few things"

***

I wake up on the cold ground. The moon above me shining down on me "I'm free" I mumble feeling the grass against my exposed skin. I walk around the dark forest something feeling off about it. The forest does not look real, I touch the trees which have shadowy whiteness around them. "Morgan. Morgan" I look around the forest until I spot two red eyes "Morgan. Morgan" it whispers. Its voice echoing throughout the forest "Morgan. Morgan" I hear a branch crack and that is when my instincts kick in and I begin to run hearing whatever running behind me too.

***

"We can't go back to the castle until we have a plan" Josh says looking back at me "We can't just run away Josh" I tell him thinking about all the places in the castle Morgan can be. "It's not running away it's called being prepared" He states driving to the nearest motel "Lets rest for now but we leave tomorrow morning. Vivian Grace is coming with us" I say hoping she finds the right ingredients for the spell. "Two bed or one" Josh asks raising a suggestive brow "Two you idiot" I say shoving him "Adeline" Josh says holding my hand which begins to tingle "Seriously" I say looking up "Awe c'mon shorty you know you wanted a piece of me since we meet" Josh says pulling me closer to him "Shut up" I mumble trying to resist my smile "So does that mean one?" I smack his arm walking ahead of him.

After arguing about the bed situation we both lay comfortably on the bed forgetting for a couple seconds about what was going on in the castle. "Here's the plan" I start to say "I will pretend to be on Jaspar's side so he won't suspect us" Josh holds my hand tightly "Shorty I just found you I can't lose you" I kiss his hand reassuring him "You won't. Promise." We both relax a bit dreading for tomorrow to come because that would mean this feeling will be over.

www.ingramcontent.com/pod-product-compliance
Lightning Source LLC
Chambersburg PA
CBHW070405200726
48294CB00003B/1097